Grandma Knows Best

Grandma
Knows
Best

From the Editors
Of *True Story* And
True Confessions

Published by True Renditions, LLC

True Renditions, LLC
105 E. 34th Street, Suite 141
New York, NY 10016

ISBN: 978-1-938877-70-4

Visit us on the web at www.truerenditionsllc.com.

Contents

THE SECRET THAT'S KILLING MY GRANDKIDS

I was floored at the sight in front of me. My twenty-five-year-old son and his three children stood huddled in my doorway.

"Can we stay with you awhile, Mom?"

"Roger!"

A bitter wind howled around the corner of the house and tried to snatch the hat from Zach's head. Zach was the youngest at two. They were all staring at me as if they had lost their best friends, or the family dog. Belatedly, I realized that while I was standing there gawking, they were slowly freezing to death. It was January in Kentucky, and we were having a very bad winter.

"Come in, come in! My God, did you drive straight through from Alabama with the kids? Where's Dallas?" I looked past him, but the sidewalk was empty, and the streetlight over my driveway revealed that the older model minivan was empty, as well.

I caught Roger's asinine look as he urged the kids inside. He was holding Zach, who looked as if he'd been crying. As he wiped his runny nose, the liquid began to run down his hand and onto the thumb he was sucking. My instincts kicked in. I grabbed the edge of my nightshirt and wiped his nose with it. His thumb made a popping sound when I took it from his mouth and cleaned it off. Then I took him from Roger, who looked exhausted.

Blair, who was six, and Kristian, who was four, shuffled in with my son. They were all bundled against the cold in several layers of clothes. I began to work at removing Zach's snowsuit, urging Blair and Kristian to do the same with their coats.

"Come on, let's get these bulky things off, then Grandma will make us all some hot cocoa. How does that sound?"

"That sounds great, Mom," Roger said, but the kids remained silent. He caught my quirked brow and mouthed silently, "Later."

Reining in my curiosity, I took them into the kitchen and set about making hot cocoa, just like my grandmother had done for me when I was a child on a cold winter's evening. I added powdered cocoa to the milk and heated it slowly. All the while I talked. I talked about the weather, and questioned the kids about the Christmas gifts I had shipped to them in December. Of course, I had already talked to them on the phone Christmas day, but I felt as if I needed to fill in the silence. In the meantime, questions filled my head.

Where was Dallas? Why didn't Roger let me know he was

1

coming? Something told me this wasn't a spur of the moment surprise visit.

Something was wrong, and I was dying to know what it was. What would possess Roger to take off with the kids and drive for hours in the dead of night? My heart lurched as another thought occurred to me. Had my son kidnapped his own children? Would he expect me to cover for him?

By the time the kids drank their hot cocoa and were tucked in my king-sized bed for the night, my mind had created all sorts of scenarios. Not a single one was pleasant.

In the kitchen again, Roger heaved a weary sigh and helped himself to another cup of cocoa. He shot me a sheepish smile when I caught him adding sugar to his cup.

"We're used to that instant stuff. It's sweeter."

I looked at the half full cups left by the kids. "Is that why they didn't drink it?"

He shrugged. "Probably. I doubt they've ever had real cocoa." His expression became shadowed with pain. "I'm sorry to barge in on you like this, Mom. Did I scare you?"

"What mother wouldn't be scared to hear the doorbell at one in the morning? Or the phone, for that matter." But I waved a hand at him. "You know it doesn't matter. You and the kids are always welcome, no matter what time of night."

Then I waited. Waited to find out what I had been dying to know since I opened the door.

Roger didn't keep me in suspense very long. "Dallas left us, Mom. She packed a suitcase and said she didn't know when she'd be back—or if she would be back at all."

I was stunned. "She—she just left her kids?"

The very idea was almost more than I could comprehend. A woman didn't leave her kids. Men left their kids—I had experience with that—but women? Not any that I knew in my lifetime. Oh, I'd watched movies, of course, and read about it in books, but I personally didn't know of anyone leaving their kids with the father and just walking out, threatening not to return.

"What on earth happened?"

Tendrils of steam rose from Roger's cup as he took a sip. When he looked at me again, his eyes were dark with anger.

"I didn't like the way she disciplined the kids. We'd been fighting about it ever since—" he broke off and started again, as if he realized he had been about to reveal too much too soon. "She finally told me I could just raise them myself."

"Oh, honey," I said, reaching out to squeeze his hand. "What she was feeling is pretty normal. Our instincts are to protect our kids, and while we may realize they need discipline, we have a hard time letting someone else do it, even if it's their father. Before he left, your dad and I—"

"Mom—" Roger interrupted gently, "You don't know what you're saying. It's not me who was being too rough with the kids. It was Dallas."

My jaw dropped again. I snapped it closed, still confused. "What do you mean, too rough?"

"She slapped Blair in the mouth," Roger said slowly, as if the words were torn out of him. "She knocked her front tooth out. Of course, she was losing it anyway, but that's not the point. She nearly choked on her tooth before we could get it out of her mouth."

Wincing, I put a hand to my own mouth, as if I could feel Blair's pain. But I was determined to be diplomatic about this.

"Roger, I know what she did was wrong, but just about every mother snaps once in a while. Don't you remember that time I dumped a whole bag of flour on Samantha's head because she said she hated me?"

"That's not abuse."

I nodded firmly. "Yes, it is. Not physical abuse, maybe, but mental abuse and just as bad." But instead of relieving Roger's pain, his face seemed to grow even paler. I felt my body stiffen with expectation, sensing there was more bad news.

"She didn't just snap, Mom. Last week she . . . she pulled a handful of hair out of Zach's head because he wouldn't get down from the kitchen table. She made his head bleed, Mom." Roger's voice grew rough and shaky. "I came home from work and saw it. When I asked her about it, she tried to lie, but Kristian told me the truth and Blair confirmed it."

I started to ask what Zach had been doing on the kitchen table, but stopped myself. What did it matter? Two-year-old kids were daring and imaginative, even I remembered that much. Whatever he'd been doing, he hadn't deserved that type of abuse from his mother or anyone else.

For lack of anything else to say, I asked, "Has she seen a doctor? Maybe she's suffering from depression or anxiety or something."

"I suggested it, but she said there was nothing wrong with her. She said it's the kids. She said she couldn't handle them, that they must have inherited some type of behavioral problem from my side of the family."

Once again, I was speechless. What happened to unconditional love? So the kids were a little rowdy. Had Dallas been abused as a child? It certainly would have been an easy excuse, but Roger anticipated my next question and answered before I could ask it.

3

"No, she wasn't abused as a child, Mom. Her parents spoiled her and her sister rotten."

"Maybe she's lying," I suggested. "Many children never tell anyone they're being abused, even when they're grown. They just block it out."

But Roger was shaking his head and starting to grow irritated with me.

"She wasn't, but even if she was, I couldn't let her abuse my kids that way. If she hadn't left, I was going to."

My next obvious question would have been why he came to me with the kids, if Dallas had been the one to leave, but I suspected I knew the answer. While he was a good father—better than most— three kids under the age of six were a handful for anyone, especially a father who worked the hours Roger normally worked at the garage. I had answered my own question, but I still had many more.

"What about the garage? Won't you get fired for taking time off?"

"I've got two weeks vacation coming up. Money's tight, but this is something I've got to do. I've got to figure out how I'm going to work things with Dallas gone. You don't mind if we stay for a bit, do you?" His wan smile held a hint of his old charm. "I could use a little help while I'm thinking. It's kinda hard to think with three kids to take care of."

"Of course I'll help you with the kids, and you can stay as long as you like."

Growing excited at the prospect—despite the sad circumstances— at the idea of spending quality time with my grandkids—I got a pad and pencil and began making a shopping list. Roger helped me, telling me their favorite cereals and snacks and what they liked to eat.

Cereals with cartoon characters on the box, snack cakes, and frozen pizzas weren't exactly what I had in mind, but I wanted them to feel at home. I smothered my protest and wrote down what they wanted. For someone who ate a lot of fresh vegetables and salads, I was a little appalled at the junk food my grandkids apparently had been eating.

But I wasn't their parent; I was the grandparent. And if there was one thing I knew about being a grandparent, it was that I had the privilege of getting to spoil them.

Breakfast the next morning was a little awkward. I hadn't had time to get to the store, so all I had on hand to prepare were eggs or oatmeal. The kids, after vetoing the eggs, settled on oatmeal, but they had a condition. They wanted a ton of brown sugar mixed in with the oatmeal.

Hiding my misgivings over how unhealthy adding all that

4

sugar seemed, I prepared the oatmeal and began making toast. I was buttering the last slice when I realized Blair was standing beside me. Roger was in the shower. I smiled down at my oldest granddaughter.

"The toast is ready," I said, expecting at least a thank you.

Blair didn't crack a smile. She said, "We don't like brown bread. We like white bread. Mom makes us white toast."

It took a few seconds to realize she was referring to the whole grain bread I was using. I bit back a smile. "But this is good for you, and it tastes good, too."

"But we don't like it."

"I don't like it, either," Kristian said from where she sat at the table.

Swallowing my hurt, I reminded myself that the kids were just being honest about what they liked. It wasn't personal. Thinking Zach wouldn't know the difference in the toast, I took him a piece along with his sweetened oatmeal. He stared down at it a moment, then picked up the toast and threw it across the room.

"No!" he shouted, startling me with the vehemence of his statement.

I fully expected the bowl of oatmeal to follow, but he merely picked up his spoon and started shoveling the food into this mouth.

"Zach doesn't like brown bread, either," Blair informed me unnecessarily. "It tastes funny."

"Oh." I managed a laugh, reminding myself that it had been some time since I'd been around kids. Apparently, there was a lot of stuff that I had forgotten.

The kids opened up to me before breakfast was over, fighting over who was going to tell me what first. Blair wanted to tell me about school. Kristian wanted to tell me about her friends, and Zach, I think, just wanted to hear his own voice. He jabbered nonstop in between bites of oatmeal. When he held out his bowl for me, I gave him another bowl and he ate that as well.

Roger came in just in time to clean up Zach and get him down from the high chair. I gathered my list and my purse and headed out the door to go shopping.

"You don't mind if we watch television?" Roger asked as Zach wiggled lose from his hold and took off at warp speed.

"Of course not," I said, pausing at the door to put on my coat. "Make yourselves at home. Oh, and there's a box of old toys in the basement, if you want to bring them up. Check for spiders before you give them to the kids."

"Will do. Thanks, Mom, for having us."

We shared a loving look before an angry shout came from the living room, and he went to check it out.

When I returned, I could hear the kids screaming before I could open the door. Thinking they were hurt, I fumbled with the lock and the sack of groceries I was holding and nearly fell into the hallway. When I got my balance, I looked into the dining area to see Roger reading the paper at the table. I knew then that there was no emergency.

But they were still screaming, and the screaming grew louder as children exploded from the living room, nearly knocking the bag of groceries from my arm.

"Watch out!" Roger shouted over the newspaper. "You nearly knocked your grandmother down!"

Without so much as a pause to show they heard their father, they continued screaming and racing around me before finally heading back into the living room. I set the bag of groceries onto the table, trying to think of a delicate way to voice my misgivings.

"Um, should they be running like that? Aren't you afraid they'll get hurt?"

Roger looked at me blankly. "What? Oh, that. They always run like that. They have a lot of energy, don't they?" He smiled as if this was something a parent should be proud of. Then his smile suddenly faltered. "Does it bother you? Because if it does, I can take them outside."

Not make them stop, but take them outside. It was freezing. "No, no. They're fine." I'll get used to it, I told myself. Never mind that my kids had never been allowed to run inside the house. It had been a house rule, and now I was starting to question myself. Had I been too hard on my kids when they were growing up? Was that why Roger was so easy on his own?

Determined not to jump to premature conclusions, I began putting away the groceries as Roger brought them inside. Kristian came tearing into the kitchen just as I was stacking the boxes of snack cakes into the cabinet.

"Can I have a cake, Grandma?"

I was so busy basking in the glow of hearing my grandchild call me Grandma that I didn't even think twice about handing her a snack cake. Then I gave one each to her siblings. It wasn't until after she'd raced out of the kitchen that I happened to glance at my watch.

Only two hours had passed since breakfast. Could they possibly be hungry? Had I forgotten that much since Roger and his sister were children? Shaking my head, I continued to put away the food.

Before I finished, Blair came skipping into the kitchen. There were crumbs around her mouth, and her remaining front tooth was black with the gummy cake when she smiled at me.

"Can we have something to drink, Grandma?" she asked.

"You certainly may," I said, smiling back at her. I reminded myself to ask Roger if he'd brought their toothbrushes as I got out the apple juice and poured three glasses. I set them on the table.

"Here you go. Grandma would really like it if you drank your juice at the table, okay? It's dangerous to carry glasses around." Especially when running at warp speed, I thought.

Grabbing a gallon of milk from the table, I opened the fridge and took a few moments rearranging things so that I could find a place for it. By the time I finished, Blair was gone, and so were the three glasses of apple juice from the table.

I stood there, debating what I should do. It was their first day. I didn't want them to start thinking I was some kind of monster. Should I ask Roger if he would make them bring the juice back to the table? And what if I hurt Roger's feelings? What if I made him feel unwelcome?

Still unsure, I went to the living room doorway, hoping to find him insisting his children take their glasses back to the dining room.

What I saw made me gasp. Zach was standing in the middle of my marble-top coffee table. It was clear by the way his knees were bent and his arms were extended, that he was about to jump to the floor. Three glasses of apple juice surrounded him.

Kristian and Blair had straddled the back of my couch and were jumping up and down furiously shouting, "Giddy up!" Apparently, they were riding imaginary horses.

Roger was nowhere in sight.

Striving to keep my voice level, I called to Zach, "No, wait, honey! Don't jump. Let Grandma get the glasses out of the—"

I was too late. Zach shot me a toothy grin and leaped over the glasses, catching the rim of one with his toe and sending it tumbling to the carpet with him. Thankfully, he wasn't hurt and the glass didn't break.

"I jumped high, Grandma!" Zach announced proudly.

"Yes, baby, you did." And nearly gave his poor grandmother a heart attack in the process. "Do you know where your daddy is?"

"Uh-uh," Zach mumbled around his thumb. He started to climb back onto the coffee table.

I grabbed his arm gently. "No, baby. Don't get on the coffee table. You're going to break your leg or something."

"We're riding broncos!" Blair shouted from her perch on the back of the sofa. "See us, Grandma?"

"Yes, yes. I see you." They were so clearly enjoying themselves I didn't have the heart to spoil their fun. In the meantime, I had let go of Zach's arm. And he was right back on the coffee table.

I quickly gathered the glasses, hoping to avert at least one catastrophe. At a loss, I turned to head back into the kitchen, thinking

I'd be better off if I didn't have to watch them doing the things they were doing.

They're at a loss. Eventually, they'll settle down, I told myself. My house was like a new playground to them.

Roger came out of the downstairs bathroom just as I was going into the kitchen. "Kids okay?"

"Well, Blair and Kristian are straddling the back of the couch, riding horses, and Zach's leaping off the coffee table."

"See? And you thought they'd be bashful." He patted my shoulder, looking suddenly sad. "They can't play like this around Dallas. She can't handle it."

The words were out before I could stop them. "Are they always this rambunctious?"

A wary look appeared in Roger's eyes. "Yeah. Why? Isn't it normal for kids to have a lot of energy?"

My throat closed up. I didn't know what to say, because I wasn't certain I'd be right. Had my kids been this rambunctious, and I just didn't remember? But they hadn't been this rowdy. This didn't seem . . . normal at all.

"Surely you're not agreeing with Dallas, that my kids aren't normal?" Roger asked with an edge to his voice.

I quickly shook my head, feeling ashamed of my thoughts. "No, no. I wasn't thinking that at all. I was thinking . . . I was thinking that maybe it's dangerous for Zach to jump off the coffee table, though."

But Roger only laughed. "He's always been a little daredevil. Daddy's little jumping bean, I call him." He put his hands on his hips, looking a lot more relaxed than he had when he arrived. "What's for lunch? Do you need any help?"

"Frozen pizza."

"Aren't you going to cook them first?" Roger teased.

I had to laugh. "Very funny, and no, I don't need any help. You just um, supervise the kids so they don't break any bones."

Material things like lamps and fragile whatnots could be replaced, I reminded myself. I winced as Zach took another leap from the coffee table, making the house shudder.

Lunch was a riot. The kids couldn't seem to sit still. They stood in their chairs, climbing from one to the other as if they had ants in their pants. More than once, I had to pull Zach down when he tried to stand up in his high chair. I was just too petrified of him falling to let him go, so eventually he got frustrated at my efforts to keep him still and started to cry.

Guilt nearly crushed me when Roger got him out of his high chair and began to rock him, soothing him with sweet words and patting his back.

"I didn't mean to make him cry," I said, losing my appetite for the salad I had made for myself.

Roger glanced up, his face expressionless. "Don't sweat it, Mom. As I'm sure you've figured out by now, they don't mind very well. Zach's just more sensitive."

"I just didn't want him to get hurt," I said miserably.

"Forget it, Mom. He has to listen once in a while." The entire time this discussion took place, Blair and Kristian had been slapping each other with their pizza. Pizza sauce splattered the white walls behind them. Their clothes and hair. I had to bite my tongue to keep from asking them to stop.

After consuming two large pizzas, the kids wanted another snack. Without hesitation, Roger got them each two snack cakes.

"Do you? . . ." I bit my lip and swallowed my words.

Roger turned to me. "Did you say something, Mom?"

"Um, no. I was about to, but then I forgot what I was going to say." It was a lie, but I had been about to ask if he really thought they needed two sugary snacks right after a big meal.

At two that afternoon, while I gathered socks and shoes and articles of clothing Zach was slowly shedding, Roger made everyone a chocolate milk shake. The kids paused long enough to suck it down. Then they continued their chase, yelling at the top of their lungs.

They had discovered how fun it was to chase each other up and down the stairs. I have to admit, I thought it was a bit strange that Roger didn't seem to think it was dangerous. But since he didn't seem to mind, I said nothing.

It wasn't until Kristian took a dangerous tumble that I took a stand. I helped him up and checked him over, then said, "That's it for, Grandma. I can't stand to see you get hurt, so you can't play on the stairs."

"Ah, man!" Kristian said with a grimace.

"Dad!" Blair yelled, pushing past me and racing to her father, who sat on the couch watching television. "Grandma won't let us play on the stairs."

I waited, my shoulders stiff with tension. At that point, I was prepared to fight Roger. The sight of Kristian tumbling head over heels down those stairs had nearly given me a heart attack.

Roger muted the television, glancing at me, then back to Blair. "Honey, if Grandma doesn't want you climbing the stairs, then you can't climb the stairs. She's probably right, anyway. It's dangerous."

"I don't like you!" Kristian announced, glaring at me. She stomped into the living room. Then she collapsed onto the floor, kicking and crying. Blair immediately joined her.

When I saw Zach edging that way, I reached out and grabbed

him, determined to defuse the situation, which had quickly gotten out of control. "Oh, no you don't, sweetheart! Grandma's got you, and I'm gonna tickle you until—"

Smack!

Zach slapped me hard in the face. I reeled with shock.

"You will sit in time out for that, little man!" Roger thundered, leaping to his feet. He marched over to me and took Zach back to the couch, sitting him in the corner.

Roger shot me an embarrassed look. "I'm sorry, Mom. I can't believe he did that." He ran an agitated hand over his face, and this time when he looked at me, he looked scared.

He knows it's not normal, what they do, I realized suddenly. He knows and he's scared. Of what? That someone will convince him to send them to a home or a hospital? Or is he afraid that I would snap like Dallas?

That night after supper, I'd had time to do some thinking while Roger battled through bathing his children upstairs. I could tell from the shrieks and thumps that they were still in high gear.

I was gathering a notepad and pencil when the children came racing downstairs and into the kitchen.

"I wanna snack before bed," Blair demanded.

Kristian and Zach added their demands.

I smiled at my beautiful grandchildren, my love for them brimming over despite the crazy day I'd had with them. Whatever was wrong wasn't their fault, I knew. I was also determined to find out the problem and fix it.

"You can have an apple," I told them firmly. "But no cakes or cookies."

There must have been something in my expression that convinced them I wasn't going to budge from my decision. Blair made a gagging gesture with her finger and turned away. Kristian, as kids are wont to do, mimicked her. Zach simply stared at me, sucking on his thumb, his big brown eyes studying me as if he couldn't quite figure me out.

An hour later, Roger put them to bed. He looked tired, wet, and irritated as he sat at the table with me.

"Maybe I didn't help Dallas enough," he admitted, looking to me for advice.

I was ready for him. Pulling the trashcan close to the table, I began to rummage through it, reading the labels on the snack cake boxes, the pizza boxes, the white bread sack, and even the apple juice label. I scribbled down numbers as I read, aware of Roger watching me as if I'd lost my mind.

During the half hour I worked in my notepad, the kids came downstairs four times. Once for water, running full steam up and down the stairs. The second time, they came down to tell me good night—again. The third time, it was to tell Roger good night again. The fourth time it was tell me that my sheets smelled good.

Up and down the stairs four times. I had been traveling those stairs for many years, and they weren't easy. I'd be out of breath just going up, and if I had to do it four times in a half an hour, I think I would probably pass out.

Granted, kids had more stamina, energy, and drive than I did, but that was still a lot of energy expended in a brief time—especially considering the energetic day they'd already had. Where did all that energy come from?

I had a growing suspicion that I knew, and the prospect of solving a very serious problem excited me. It wasn't something I had just invented, I knew. It was just something I had never taken very seriously, as I suspect a lot of people hadn't.

"Mom. Are you going to tell my why you're going through the trash?" Roger finally asked me.

Since I was finished anyway, I told him. "I'm writing down how many carbohydrates and sugars each of the kids had today."

My son slapped his forehead. "God. Tell me you're not on one of those wacky low-carb diets."

"No, I'm not, but don't knock it until you've tried it. Remember Wilma Remington?"

"Your church buddy?"

"Yes, her. She lost a hundred pounds on a low-carb diet, and she's never been healthier."

"But I thought kids needed a lot of carbohydrates."

"They do, but there's the bad kind, and the good kind. For instance; the carbs in an apple are good carbs. The carbs in a snack cake are bad carbs."

"Oh."

I tallied my numbers and turned the pad around so that he could view it. "See?"

He studied it a moment, then his eyebrows rose. "Hey, even I can see that's a lot of sugar. Did they really have that much?"

I nodded. "The disturbing part is a portion of that sugar came from the apple juice."

"Wow. Is that why they stay hungry all the time?"

"Yes. The sugar from one snack cake," I paused to give him a stern look from beneath my brows, "or two sends their blood sugar soaring. Their bodies immediately produce insulin to convert the sugar to glucose, but with so much sugar, the pancreas produces too much insulin. That sends their blood sugar too low, which triggers their hunger. It's a vicious cycle. I watched a documentary on television

11

one night about this. Experts predict that one out of every three kids born in 2004 will become a diabetic. They also had this special where they put this theory to the test at a school for kids with behavioral—even violent—problems. They took out the sugar and bad carbs and sodas and junk and fed them only good food. There was a remarkable difference in their behavior."

I tapped my pencil against my notebook, frowning as a new thought occurred to me. "I wonder how many kids diagnosed with ADHD really have it? What if some of them are simply getting too much sugar?"

Roger leaned forward. I could tell I definitely had his attention. "Mom, if you're right, this could change everything. It might even save my marriage."

To be perfectly fair, I had to say, "I could be wrong, son. Let's don't count our chickens before they hatch, okay? Let's put it to the test over the next week."

"I'm with you. God, if you're right. . . ." He leaned his head on his arm, and then looked back at me, clearly upset. "Mom, the truth is, I think my kids are out of control, too. But I just couldn't stand Dallas abusing them."

"I don't blame you, son," I said softly. "But you know what they say . . . the first step is admitting you have a problem." I grinned and he laughed.

He quickly sobered, offering me an apologetic look. "I'm sorry, Mom, for bringing this on you. I really didn't know where else to turn. I try to make them mind, but they act as if they don't even hear me. It was driving Dallas crazy, I guess. I should have been honest with you instead of letting you think I just let my kids do anything they want."

"I think I was close to figuring it out," I said dryly. I stood up and started throwing cakes and cookies into the trash. Roger got up to help.

"Isn't this wasteful?" he asked, watching me throw the frozen junk food on top of the cookies.

"If I knew someone to give it to, I would, but the store won't take it back and I don't want either of us to be tempted when the kids start begging."

Roger froze. "They'll start begging?"

"They might actually suffer from sugar withdrawals."

"No kidding?"

"No kidding." Finished clearing out the kitchen of junk food, I grabbed the notepad again and sat down. "Now it's time to make a new list . . . and put your tough love hat on. Thank God for our twenty-four hour super center."

"Amen," Roger said with such feeling, I had to laugh.

The first day of our test didn't go well, but then I hadn't expected it that it would. It was filled with tantrums and screams because the kids wanted cereal instead of eggs or plain oatmeal, snack cakes instead of fruit or cheese. When I served them baked fish and steamed vegetables, you would have thought I had laid a freshly skinned cow in front of them.

They didn't eat breakfast at all, but by lunchtime they grudgingly ate their sandwiches on whole grain bread.

Zach turned traitor and ate an entire plate of carrot sticks with ranch dressing. He even asked for more.

By three in the afternoon, Blair came to the table and sat down in front of the apple wedges with peanut butter I had left out. I could feel her glaring at me, but I hid my smile.

While I pretended to clean the sink, she ate every one of them. Kristian joined her before she was finished and ate hers as well. They drank their milk, and took an orange from the fruit bowl into the living room.

Zach didn't stand up in his high chair. He didn't scream or bang his spoon or try to rock through the wall.

By supper, the older kids were still pretending they hated us, but they were oddly . . . normal. That's all I can say. They were normal kids. They got a little rowdy for about a half hour before bedtime, but I remembered that it wasn't unusual.

After they went to bed, Roger and I didn't hear one single peep out of them. In fact, he was so concerned by their silence, he made several trips upstairs to see if they were okay.

Wearing a dazed expression, he joined me at the table. I was enjoying a leisurely cup of decaf and trying not to smile like the cat that ate the canary—or the Grandma who tamed her grandkids.

"I don't believe it! They're sound asleep, and Zach hasn't even kicked off his covers, like he normally does."

"Hmm."

"They didn't even need any water," Roger continued to muse out loud.

"Less salt in fruit and vegetables."

When Roger looked at me, I saw that he had tears in his eyes. "Mom, you are the smartest woman I know. I love you."

I had to blink my eyes to clear my vision. "I love you, too, but I'm not really that smart, son. I read a lot, watch a lot of television, and I'm curious about things."

"Thank God that you are!" Roger blew out a long, shaky sigh. "I'm almost afraid to go to sleep, afraid I'll wake up and this will have been a dream." His eyes were huge as he glanced at me again. "Are you sure today just isn't a fluke or something?"

13

I shrugged, but I was pretty confident it wasn't. "I guess we'll see, won't we?"

And we did. The next day, the kids ate a full breakfast of bacon, eggs, and whole grain toast. I had managed to find some orange juice containing a third less sugar, and gave each of them a small glass. They sipped it, ate their breakfast, and didn't move from their chairs.

I had to keep covering my mouth to hide my smile at Roger's astonished expression. After breakfast, I put on a children's movie for Blair and Kristian, and Zach settled in the floor to push around some of Roger's old toy trucks.

After the movie Blair and Kristian played hide and seek. They did run once or twice, and they did get the giggles, as kids will do, but it was so different from the wild, all-out screaming and running. Now they were listening when we spoke to them, and because their brains weren't racing a mile a minute from a sugar overload, they heard what we said. And most of the time, they did what they were told.

Roger kept muttering, "I can't believe this. I can't believe this."

The rest of the week went pretty much the same. Roger and I were both enjoying the kids in a way we couldn't have before.

On Saturday, I answered the door to find Dallas standing on the threshold, looking forlorn and miserable. "Dallas," I said quietly, not sure how I should feel about her desertion. Part of me understood, but there was another part of me that still couldn't believe she had done it—no matter how bad her kids were.

"You probably hate me," she said. Then she burst into tears.

I pulled her inside and hugged her as she cried, my heart melting like butter left in the hot sun. I knew Dallas wasn't a bad mother or a bad wife. How could I not know it, after I'd witnessed how terrible the kids had been?

Finally, she pulled back and found some tissues in her coat pocket. She blew her nose nosily. "I've been going to a counselor," she confessed. "I—I just couldn't come back until I knew I wasn't going to hit my kids again."

We had another crying session before she realized she didn't hear the kids. She looked terror stricken. "Oh my God! Where are they? I thought he'd come here. . . ."

My smile nearly split my face in two. "They are here," I told her. "They're in the living room watching a movie." I could tell from her expression that she didn't believe me, so I took her hand and walked her to the living room doorway.

The scene couldn't have been lovelier if I had painted it.

Zach sat at Roger's feet, pushing cars up his leg and watching them fall. His delighted laughter made Dallas gasp back a sob. Blair and Kristian lay on the floor in front of the television.

14

Tears rolled down Dallas's face. She turned her stunned, bewildered gaze to my smiling face. "What did you . . . why are they . . . was it me?"

"No, no," I hastened to assure her. "Roger and I will explain it to you later. Don't you want to say hi to your kids?"

For a moment, a look of pure terror washed over her face. I was reminded that she had left her husband and kids, and she didn't know how she would be received. Well, I decided she'd have to work that one out on her own.

And she did. She walked into the room until Roger caught sight of her. "Dallas!" he exclaimed, a smile breaking across his face. He jumped to his feet, and suddenly Dallas was covered in kisses and kids and a very happy husband.

I'm back to seeing my grandkids every so often, but I hear regular reports about their progress. Roger and I made a believer out of Dallas, and she's continuing to keep their sugar level down.

I don't know if my grandkids were super sensitive to sugar, or if they really were just getting too much. I think everyone who believes sugar overload might be a problem should probably consult their doctors and pediatricians before testing this theory, but I wouldn't be surprised if those doctors and pediatricians all agree that we, as a nation, eat entirely too much junk food—especially junk food containing processed sugar.

My mind is full of what ifs. What if the kid down the street who throws rocks at your dog and terrorizes other kids is getting too much sugar? What if the kid who can't concentrate in school and can't sit still isn't ADHD, but eating too much sugar? A hundred years ago, the average person ate a pound of sugar a year. Now the average person eats one hundred pounds of sugar a year.

It's scary who we've become. But the great thing is that we can change—just the way my grandkids did!

THE END

"I PRAYED TO GOD FOR GRANDMA— 'PLEASE DON'T TAKE MY SUNSHINE AWAY!' "

She was one of those special ladies—the kind of grandma you never forget

I wrote a poem about my grandmother just a few weeks before she died. My dad called to tell me that Mame—or, as she spelled it, Maym—my grandmother, his mother, was in the hospital. It seemed like she wouldn't be there very long and the doctors were optimistic that she'd be able to go home soon.

They were right. She did go home.

But something in me knew, even then, that it was the beginning of the end.

I broke down crying while my husband held me. I remember thinking that I was being overdramatic, but a small, knowing part inside began gently preparing for what was to come.

When I was little, my family was my whole world. Until I was five, I lived in an apartment complex that had no other children living there. I grew up having dinner at Maym and Papa's once a week. I can remember the scent of her kitchen. There was never any takeout or ordering of food at her house. She cooked all the food on her own and we always sat down as a family to eat.

Maym was a stickler for good manners while eating. No elbows were allowed to seek a restful solace on the table, no talking with your mouth full, no interrupting unless you first said, "Excuse me," and no leaving the table until everyone was finished. I remember thinking, at four years old, that dinners at Maym's had to be the longest dinners in the world!

After the plates were cleared we'd adjourn to the sitting room and the adults would talk over coffee. But most times, Maym and I would sing together. It is in great part due to Maym that my love of singing took shape, playing the piano right there in her living room. I remember the first time I heard Judy Garland sing. I thought it was my grandmother singing! There are pictures of me sitting on the wooden stool next to her, trying to play a tambourine while Maym sang and played the piano. Maym sang Christmas carols in the spring, songs from the 1940s, nursery rhymes, and her favorite song for me, "You

16

Are My Sunshine." That was her nickname for me, "Sunshine," and besides singing with her, playing cards was our favorite pastime. Maym loved to be the center of attention and I loved being next to her.

I suppose it's not surprising, then, that I started doing musical theatre and belted my heart out at the age of ten. I performed all through high school and then majored in musical theatre in college. Maym was at my graduation. She'd stopped playing the piano by then, because it was too painful. The arthritis made her hands swollen and difficult to move.

Maym was the epitome of a southern belle hostess, even though she was born in Yugoslavia and lived in New York City until she moved to Louisville, Kentucky in her thirties. There was something about southern hospitality that really appealed to her. It was a trait that she never lost, even feigning a southern accent sometimes. She felt it was a warmer, gentler way to converse.

As a child I was encouraged to call her Maym instead of the traditional "Grandmother" for two reasons. One was that she'd already acquired the nickname Auntie Mame from her nieces and nephews, and the other being that when I was born, she felt that she was "much too young to be a 'grandmother,' " so Maym was her choice and it just stuck. My younger sister and cousins also called her Maym, and even some of the neighborhood children kept up the tradition. It was a name that suited her.

Maym was fast and smart and could match wits and hold her own with the best of them. It seemed she held two degrees, one in sarcasm and one in bad puns. I remember how she smelled when I hugged her because Maym wore the same perfume all her life, even before I was born. She never changed her scent. Maym said she kept the same perfume so that when any member of the family smelled another woman wearing her perfume, we would instantly be reminded of her. Her plan would take effect when one of us was innocently shopping at the supermarket or walking absentmindedly in a department store. When we smelled it, WHAM! Maym. She was a smart lady. It always worked.

Maym and Papa moved away when I was five years old, and I remember walking through their living room packed with boxes stacked taller than I, feeling heavy, knowing even then that life would be forever different. As I grew up I saw her less and less, mostly at holidays and such. I have small, disjointed memories of those visits: Maym and I playing cards, her throaty laugh when she was really amused, or how she helped me with my vocabulary words. To this day, I know how to spell together because of how she broke it down as "to-get-her."

When Maym went into the hospital a second time, my husband

and I went to visit. If it was going to be the end, I wanted to be there to say good-bye and make sure that Maym knew how much I loved her and how much she meant to me. That just isn't fully conveyed over a thin phone line. The sound of my voice would be too little a gift. I wanted to be there in the room with her, even if she wasn't sure who I was. I felt that deep down she would know and if she didn't, then I would.

I found her room and stood outside, peering around the open door to get a glimpse of how she looked. The person I saw in that bed did not look like my grandmother. It felt like someone was instantly squeezing me too tightly. I had to take a step back from that uncomfortable embrace and just breathe. With my breath came tears, but I held them back.

Maym was lying on her side, appearing to sleep, but it was not a normal, relaxed sleep. Her hair was slicked back to her head in a way I'd never seen before and instead of looking old and worn out, she looked unnaturally young—not a wrinkle on her face, it seemed. She'd always filled any room, but there, in a bed too white and too large for her, the room devoured her. I stepped through the doorway and told her that I was there. Her eyes flashed open in recognition. I was certain Maym knew I was there, even if it was difficult for her to communicate that.

That flash of a moment is what I hold onto tightly when I miss her a little too much, or when it hurts a little more than I'd like, knowing that no more letters addressed to My Darling Sunshine will grace my mailbox.

It seems grandparents are forever on the outskirts of a grandchild's life—attending graduations and recitals, sending presents for birthdays and holidays—and as a child, you feel like they do all this because they're required to. This is what grandparents do. This is their job, to take care of you when your parents go out of town, or buy you the toy you want just because you asked. It never occurs to you that perhaps they want to be there, that they love you so much that they sit through the "obligatory" five-hour recital for one reason: They love you just that much.

Grandparents remember your birthday every year because the day you were born is just as special to them as it is to your parents. Grandparents get to see you as perfect from Day One and just keep on believing that. I hope that my grandmother did. I never doubted that she loved me and always wanted the best for me. I just remember all the letters that she sent, the times she cried because I sang in a play, or simply showed up to visit.

Those times flooded back to me as I stood next to a sterile hospital bed holding my grandmother's hand. My whole family came back the following weekend to visit, and Maym died that Monday. My grandmother had her family around her, telling stories and laughing through the sadness in her last days. I felt proud and blessed to be there, to have been born into a family that is truly in every essence of that word—a family.

Everyone says in times like this that it's "hard" and "difficult," and that is undeniably true. But along with the sadness and the difficulty, I felt love—love from my parents, my grandfather, my husband, and from Maym. It didn't matter that she couldn't speak to us. Her family spoke for her. There was laughter and joy in that room. That is what moved me and helped me through the weekend. That is the only thing that mattered. You could only take love and lightness into her hospital room, because anything else you took would just make the experience low and ugly, and those are things my grandmother was not.

In the months that have passed since Maym died, I find myself thinking of her more than I predicted I might. We spoke less and less as I grew older, only on holidays and the occasional "just thinking about you" phone calls here and there. She was not as much a part of my daily life, or so I thought. But the smallest object, scent, or song will immediately take me back to her laugh, her kitchen, or her hands on the piano. All of those images that were probably always there, but I brushed by them knowing we would make more memories. Now all I have are those vivid memories and I am grateful to have known my grandmother, and grateful that she had such an impact on my childhood and on my life.

While we were out shopping recently, my husband and I were talking about Maym and as we were talking, an older, gray-haired woman wearing Maym's perfume brushed by me. I laughed to myself and then had to explain to my husband what I found so amusing. He laughed with me. I smelled like my grandmother's hug for the rest of the day. I didn't want to take a shower because I enjoyed reveling in Maym's scent so much.

Maym was special. She was special because she was mine. She was special simply because she was my grandmother. I loved her then and I love her now, and that will sustain me throughout my lifetime. No one can ever take that from me. No one can ever take my sunshine away.

THE END

GARAGE SALE OF
THE CENTURY
I got more than I bargained for

I was waiting on my front stoop, barely into my first cup of coffee, when my grandmother's car rumbled to the curb.

Beep! Beep!

Before I had time to cross the yard, she laid on the horn again. "Come on, sweetie," she said, rolling down the driver's side window. "Time's a-wasting!"

"Good heavens, Gran." I pushed aside a pile of bingo chips and settled into the front seat. "What's the rush?"

"You need a dress, that's the rush. And I intend to find you one if we have to hit every sale on this list." She tapped the classified section of the newspaper that poked out of her bright orange tote bag, which was the same color as her hair. Gran had no intention of growing old gracefully.

"Sometimes I'm not sure if you're my grandmother or my fairy godmother," I said, smiling at her. The truth was, Gran had been like a mother to me since my mother had died when I was twelve.

We chatted easily as we drove along that beautiful May morning. When an old song came on the radio, we sang along—loudly and off-key.

"I just love spring cleaning," Gran said when the song ended. I had a fleeting image of her little apartment, which was crammed from floor-to-ceiling with clutter—years worth of magazines, bright skeins of yarn, some two hundred odd salt and pepper shakers.

I cracked a smile. "Since when?"

"Not mine, silly. Other people's. Honestly, there's just no accounting for what people will give away." She grinned mischievously. "Especially where we're going."

She swung onto the parkway, and soon we were cruising through the fanciest neighborhood in town. I slunk down in my seat as Gran's car barged down the boulevard, feeling as conspicuous as if Gran had been flashing the headlights or blaring the horn.

Our first two stops turned up nothing but old vases and dog-eared paperbacks.

"The day's still young," Gran chirped, tucking a romance novel into her tote bag.

"I hope I'm going to find a dress," I said wistfully.

What would the sales girls at Dixie's say if they could see me now? I thought. An assistant manager shopping for a dress at a rich woman's yard sale. Even with my promotion, it takes every cent I earn just to get my bills paid.

"You can always wear the pink one with the black polka dots," Gran said. "All the girls commented on how sweet you looked at the church social last week."

"Oh, Gran!" I wailed. "I can't wear that dress to my boss's wedding!"

"Who are you going with, dear?" she asked, bringing the conversation around to her favorite subject—my love life.

"Uhm," I hesitated, then, hoping I sounded convincing, I said, "I haven't decided yet."

"You don't mean you don't have a date?" She gaped at me as if the idea were unthinkable. "That nice young man who calls the numbers at my bingo still asks after you."

Why wouldn't he? I thought. He took me to the most expensive restaurant in town and then stuck me with the bill.

"How about Estelle's nephew, Karl?" she said hopefully. "He's a banker, you know."

"But Gran, he's twice my age."

"It's not as though you're getting any younger, dear."

I bit back an angry reply, reminding myself that she was only trying to help. In Gran's day, being twenty-six and single made you an old maid. But this was the new millennium. Women had more options now. And besides, the kind of man I wanted only seemed to exist in romance novels and fairy tales.

"Uh oh," I said, cutting Gran off. "I think we just passed a sale."

Gran threw the car into reverse. As we stared up at the three-storey Queen Anne-style house, I could tell that even Gran, who was an experienced "saler" in rich waters, was impressed. I trailed behind, admiring a bed of tulips, as Gran's heels clicked in a no-nonsense way up the walk. She followed the yard sale signs to the backyard, flung open the gate, and barged straight into the path of the most beautiful man I'd ever seen. When he and Gran collided, the bucket of water he'd been carrying sloshed over onto the front of his shirt.

"Good heavens!" Gran exclaimed.

"Are you all right, ma'am?" the man asked. His voice was deep and sexy, slightly southern.

"I'm fine, dear," Gran said breathlessly. "But I'm afraid I've gone and spoiled your shirt."

"No harm done," he said with an easy laugh.

My eyes sprinted from his sun-streaked hair to his big, bronzed arms, obviously the product of hours on the golf course.

"Ah, I was just going to give my flowers a drink."

21

I realized I was still standing in his path and quickly moved aside, hoping he hadn't noticed my staring. "They're lovely," I stammered, feeling my face turn red. "You're gardens, I mean."

"Thanks." He smiled. It was the kind of smile that could send a girl into a trance.

"Why don't you put on some lipstick, dear?" Gran whispered loudly. The spell shattered. I hurried across the porch, sure that by now my face was the color of his tulips.

We walked past tables piled high with dishes, puzzles, and paperback novels.

The usual, I thought with disappointment, nothing I haven't seen already today.

And then I saw the dresses. Racks and racks of them—satins, velvets, silks. They all smelled faintly of patchouli, and all were size eight. My breath caught in my throat. I would've liked to bury my face in their luxurious folds, but I noticed that the yard sale man was watching me.

"Looking for a dress?" he asked pleasantly.

I shrugged. "Maybe."

"She's got some pretty ones there," he said.

You're telling me, I thought. This guy must be loaded if his wife can afford to sell gowns like these for five bucks apiece. She probably just got tired of them. I bet she's out at the boutique right now restocking her closet.

I pulled an elegant silver dress from the rack and hugged it to me.

"So." Gran's eyes twinkled as they slid to the man running the yard sale. "Are there any other wishes I can grant for you, my dear?" she asked me.

I marched away, my face on fire again, still clutching the dress. While Gran sorted through the paperbacks, I plowed through a mountain of shoes. I held my breath as I slipped my feet into a pair of slingbacks.

"Look, Gran," I whispered, "it's as though they were made for me." But Gran was on the other side of the patio, laughing it up with the yard sale man, like they were old friends.

I smiled, happy to see Gran enjoying herself. Then I had a horrifying thought. "That's my granddaughter, Sloane," I could almost hear her saying. "She's still single, the poor thing. I don't suppose you have a brother—" I bolted across the porch, but she was only haggling over the price of a purple sweater.

"I guess we're ready to check out, dear," she said to the man. I couldn't take my eyes off of his hands as he tallied our purchases and carefully folded them into paper grocery bags. Callused hands, I noted with surprise. I'd have thought this was the home of a surgeon or a

22

corporate executive. My eyes swept across the million-dollar lawn.

"What a lovely home you have," I said wistfully. "I dream of gardens like these."

"I can't take any credit for the house," he said, handing me a business card, "but if you're serious about your gardens, give me a call. I have excellent references."

I stared at him dumbly. "You mean, you're the gardener?"

He laughed. "That's right. I was here to do some irrigating this morning when Mrs. Hartwell's daughter, Lili, broke her arm. I'm just filling in at the yard sale while they're at the hospital." He extended a big, gentle hand. "I'm Tim."

"Sloane Wilson," I said. I shook his hand without meeting his eyes.

"Call any time, Sloane."

"I'll do that." My hand trembled as I pocketed his card.

Gran smiled knowingly as we got back into her car. "I don't hold with this business of girls calling boys," she said, trying to sound stern. "But I do think those window boxes of yours could use a helping hand."

"Oh Gran, I could never—"

"Hey, Sloane?"

I looked up. Tim ran across the yard, carrying the shoes. "You forgot your shoes." He leaned into the open window and deposited them onto my lap. He smelled of fresh air and sunshine.

"Listen, even if you don't need a gardener, I'd still like for you to call. We could have dinner," he offered.

"Oh," I said, floundering badly, "I, uhm . . ."

He smiled at me again. "I'm a pretty nice guy. Like I said, you can check my references."

I laughed, suddenly at ease. I told him I'd call him soon, and this time I meant it.

Gran was grinning from ear to ear as we pulled away, probably thinking about the great story she'd have to tell at the next church social. "That's what I love about yard sales," she said, tucking her new purple sweater into her tote bag. "There's just no telling what a girl might find."

THE END

GRANDMA'S GUMPTION
To this day, she remains one of the most
unforgettable women I've ever known

It was a hot, sultry night in my grandmother Loretta's Bronx apartment when, as a three-year-old, I took Loretta's shot of whiskey off the kitchen table and drank it.

I flapped my hand as if fanning my mouth and repeated, "Hot! Hot!" to Loretta, who screamed to my mother, "Oh, jeez, Gina—Joey drank my whiskey—he drank my dang whiskey!"

Grandma Loretta retrieved the milk that sat next to her Schaeffer beer in the small refrigerator and made me drink it to settle my stomach, and like Loretta—

I held my liquor.

Watching my grandmother drink hard liquor and beer made her very different, in my young eyes, from the other tea-drinking grandmothers that I knew, and I always derived a certain satisfaction when telling my friends about her. I liked believing that I came from a tough lineage—one that was hard and poor, but resolute all the way.

Loretta was a small and thin woman, possessing a calm, focused gaze that even as a child, dominated every photograph ever taken of her, regardless of who else was in it. My grandfather, Vito Carleoni, Sr., called Loretta "Bedroom Eyes."

Actually, there's no justice in calling Loretta different—unparalleled is more like it.

Born Loretta Lombardi on March 16, 1914 in Harlem, New York, Loretta was a whiskey-drinking hell-raiser with a volatile personality that earned her the nickname "Mommy Dearest," after Joan Crawford. Loretta once took a handful of aspirin because she disagreed with my mother's first marriage and the resident psychiatrist at Jacobi Hospital diagnosed Grandma Loretta with hysterical personality disorder.

Loretta birthed three children, survived tuberculosis and breast cancer, and held a family together through a decade of hard times and welfare—all complicated by the mental instabilities suffered by Grandpa Vito, whom she eventually lost to cancer in September 1971. Two weeks later, Loretta's brother, Luigi, nicknamed "Luigi Long Shoes," suffered a fatal heart attack. A year and a half after that trying September, Loretta suffered another loss.

John Carleoni was the oldest of Loretta's three children and he resembled a Fifties version of Johnny Depp, with slicked-back hair

24

and a thick pompadour on top of his head. He loved drinking pots of coffee and chain-smoking Chesterfields.

In May of 1973, John visited with his friend and best man, Angelo. It was a spring gathering of friends and a little baseball. After playing ball, John settled in for his favorite dish of tomato sauce with rigatoni and cheese. When John finished his supper, he drank a customary nip of crème de menthe and complained of weakness and exhaustion. His friends ribbed him that he couldn't handle his liquor, but John shrugged it off and went into Angelo's bedroom to lie down.

A few minutes later, his seven-year-old daughter, Carmen Louise, checked on John and heard what Loretta recalled as "the death rattle"—a rear-throated breathing sound that emanates from a person in the last moments of life. Loretta's oldest son died of a massive heart attack on his best man's bed at the age of thirty-six.

I was barely a toddler during that time, and although very dear relatives died, the family moved on and traditions continued—good and bad traditions.

Loretta loved her liquor throughout the hardships of her life and beyond, which contributed to a tumultuous relationship between Loretta and my mother. Loretta's usual libations consisted of boilermakers: a shot of Seagram's whiskey followed by her favorite, Schaeffer beer. This zealous habit made for electric moments.

I remember one Fourth of July evening when Loretta erupted at our country home so furiously that she was the fireworks display. It started with my sister, Gina, deciding to rest her infant son, Anthony, on a blanket on the grass.

Old Bronx Loretta feared the country because of its "mysterious, creepy" inhabitants. Loretta sat in a lawn chair, sipping her firewater and staring down at baby Anthony.

"How can you put that baby on the ground with all these bugs and things crawling around, Gina?"

My sister assured her that everything was fine, no need to worry. But Loretta pressed further. Finally, my sister told Loretta, "Don't worry about the baby, Grandma; I can handle it."

That was it. Loretta ruminated and the antebellum was short-lived. She stormed into the house and yelled at my mother, who was in the kitchen getting ready to bring out a pot of fresh coffee.

"You should be ashamed of yourself, Giovanna!"

"Ashamed of what, Ma?" my mother asked.

"Ashamed of yourself for raising such a disrespectful child, that's for what!"

My Aunt Philomena, Loretta's older sister, pleaded with Loretta to settle down. Philomena knew what was coming. But the tension accumulated and when night fell, Mount Loretta blew, screaming about

25

anything and everything to anyone who would—or wouldn't—listen.

Fearing the worst, my mother's older brother, Vito, Jr., huddled our Bronx relatives into his car for the trip back to the city. Although a lapse in the relationship followed, love prevailed and I soon found myself back in the car, headed for Sunday trips to the Bronx.

Whenever we drove to Loretta's apartment, I pleaded with my parents to stop at White Castle for their delicious miniature hamburgers. With the exception of Yankee Stadium, for me, White Castle was the epitome of the Bronx. I didn't always get my way because filling up on hamburgers at White Castle inevitably left the family open to an attack from Loretta, who, like a clever old fox, exposed our indulgence and tore into us for not saving our appetites for her usual supper of veal and potatoes.

If the family was content sitting in Loretta's hotbox, I knew I was in for a day of boredom and pacing, which inevitably led to Loretta menacing me with a wooden sauce spoon for being too fidgety. I once snatched the sauce spoon off the stove and threw it off Loretta's fire escape into the courtyard below . . . and then sucked in my breath, anticipating a slap from my grandmother. Sometimes, though, the cosmos aligned just right and something I did that would normally have incited a scolding provided everyone with laughs, instead.

We often took Loretta to St. Raymond's Cemetery in Throgs Neck to visit Grandpa Vito and Uncle Johnny's graves. My older sister, Gina, always cried as we stood before their headstones, but since I was an infant when they died, I didn't quite join in the sadness. In fact, one Memorial Day weekend while my sister was her usual gushy self, I ran around stealing flags off the veterans' graves, not having any concept of why they were there. When Loretta saw what I was doing, she "explained" to me why I should not steal the flags and then I cried, too—no wooden spoon needed.

Sometimes Loretta would stare at Grandpa Vito's headstone and say, "Yeah, Vito, you finally got to ride in a Cadillac," referring to Grandpa Vito's hearse. My grandfather's lifelong dream was to own a Cadillac, a quixotic state of mind considering the family finances, so I promised Loretta that I'd buy her a Cadillac when I grew up to fulfill what Grandpa Vito was never able to do. Thereafter, my "Cadillac promise" remained a subject of amusement around Loretta's dinner table, probably because Loretta knew that she'd be long gone before I could do anything for her about a Cadillac.

When darkness approached the city, I always knew that the end of our visit with Loretta was near. I would lean on a windowsill that was thick with layers of lead paint and look out past the fire escape to Westchester Avenue, waiting for the blue neon sign of the Ortez Funeral Home to come on.

The Ortez letters would brighten as the horizon changed from cobalt blue to a blanket of night covering the Bronx. Warm air radiating off brick and pavement would intermingle with smells from the streets and flirt with the damp iron fire escape before wafting past me into Loretta's apartment. I would smell that air and watch people walking in and out of the courtyard below, but the glowing Ortez sign always pulled me back, and I would know then that a feeling was coming.

Loretta would sit at the table with my parents recalling happier times as an evanescent loneliness would creep into me like a quiet, gathering fog. In my mind, Loretta's voice fused with the glowing neon sign, bringing a haunting loneliness that I believed Loretta felt, too, and I always carried that feeling with me to the elevator after exchanging good-byes with Loretta.

As we'd head for the car, Loretta would wave to us from her third-floor window. I would think about her alone in that hot apartment as we drove home and everything in my mind would turn blue: my mood, the Ortez sign, the profound blue veins on Loretta's old hands, and the bluish-gray smoke I imagined floating from her True Blue cigarettes.

In January of 1989, doctors at Jacobi Medical Center in the Bronx discovered three clogged arteries leading to Loretta's heart. In February, at the age of seventy-five, she underwent triple bypass surgery. Afterward, Loretta spent five days at Albert Einstein Medical Center and then went home.

Eight months later, doctors informed Loretta that recent blood tests had revealed that she had T-cell leukemia. Although Loretta didn't feel sick, the psychosomatics of her situation played tricks on her mind.

From that point on, she was in and out of the hospital for the next two years and in 1992, Loretta's body finally weakened. Worn out and run-down from stress and bacterial pneumonia, Loretta spent all but one week of the last six months of her life at Jacoby Hospital and Albert Einstein Medical Center in the Bronx.

I was twenty-one when Loretta entered the hospital for the last time. I went to visit her and winced when I saw the blotches of black and blue that covered her body. Loretta's timeworn skin resembled the delicacy of a dragonfly's wings and looked susceptible to the cruel tearing of a child. The slightest touch bruised Loretta and a needle shot turned a large portion of her arm dark purple.

Though abrasive, Loretta persisted in being the grandmother I knew and loved. She referred to her cardiologist as "lemon puss" because he never smiled, and with a rotund nurse present, she observed my mother's silhouette against the window and greeted her

27

with, "Oh, my God—you're fat—and getting fatter!"

The nurse turned to my mother and said, "And thank you for driving seventy miles to come see me today, my lovely daughter."

The young physicians' assistants liked Loretta for her smart mouth. When a burly PA named Bostwick told Loretta that he was going skiing for the weekend, she replied by telling him that he was only going so he could "get lucky in the snow"—this coming from a seventy-eight-year-old woman! Another PA whom Loretta referred to as Dennis the Menace, told her that she couldn't die because the wicked go on forever.

In June of 1992, the bad blood in Loretta's mind and body tightened its grip, worsening the pain in her head and limbs. On June 16, Dr. Kendall explained to my mother that one of two things could happen: leave Loretta in her present state, or increase the morphine to kill the pain, which would also slow Loretta's heart—the latter being an intimate understanding between Dr. Kendall and my parents. My mother optioned to increase the morphine and from that point on, the family watched Loretta's body anesthetize itself. On June 17, 1992, Loretta died of congestive heart failure.

Today, as I recognize just how different and unique Loretta truly was, I wish that I appreciated her differences earlier in life. My mother tells me that appreciation comes with age, and maybe that's true. I just wish that I could have bought Loretta that Cadillac, even though she never drove a day in her life.

THE END

A Reader's Heart-Wrenching Devotion:
GRANDMA TO THE RESCUE!
I did it all to spare my grandbaby from suffering

I sat on the old sofa in the back of my beauty shop, mulling over the difficult day I'd had. Patty, my best beautician and friend, handed me a cup of coffee.

"Looks like you could use this, Connie," she said as she sat down beside me with a groan. "This sure was a rough Saturday and I am beat!"

I nodded. "It sure didn't help that two of the girls called in sick. What am I going to do with those girls? Did you hear all those complaints from the customers? It was just impossible to squeeze in their appointments, too. A few more days like this and I'll be out of business!"

"Oh, Connie, the girls are young. We all know they weren't really sick." Patty patted my knee. "These things happen and those same customers who complained will be back again next week."

I sighed. "I've had this shop for three years and I'm finally starting to see a profit here and I'd hate to lose it. This shop is all I have."

Patty nodded. "Go home, Connie. Take a hot bath, have a glass of wine, and relax. You'll feel better next week."

I hesitated, looking around the messy shop. Patty read my mind.

"I'll clean up, now go!" she ordered, and I had to laugh.

"Okay, Mother!" I teased.

What would I do without a good friend like Patty?

As I drove home I thought about my past and all the events that led me into buying the beauty salon. When my husband, Ed, died four years ago I knew I needed a drastic change. For years, I'd had my beautician's license tucked away, never really making any use of it. While raising our daughter, Jordan, I never considered an outside job. Ed's job more than paid the bills and I did beauty work at home for friends and a few relatives and that was enough for me.

We had a good life until Jordan started high school. For a while, we thought it was just a phase. Jordan started to hang around with a rough crowd, cut school often, and she broke our rules many, many times. We worried about her constantly and Ed and I argued a lot about how to discipline her. When Jordan began her junior year, we hoped that things would get better and at first, she really seemed to make an effort; she joined an after-school activity and started to pull up her grades and she even started talking about college. Then one evening, she came home and told us that she was pregnant. Our world fell apart after that.

I think Ed took it harder than I did. Jordan was determined to keep her baby, even if the young father was not willing to help. He ran off and joined the service, leaving our daughter all alone to raise their child. There were many tears and arguments that year for all of us. Ed and I blamed ourselves; we wondered many times if we'd failed our daughter as parents.

On top of everything else, Ed's company was in trouble and he was let go right before our granddaughter, Alicia, was born. I kept telling him that we would manage, but the financial burden of Jordan's pregnancy and delivery kept us both up at night. Ed tried so hard, but finding a new job at his age was no easy task. I considered going to work myself, but Ed wouldn't hear of it.

However, once Alicia was born, all the tears and terrible words just melted away. Ed just loved that baby; he told me that he'd been given a second chance with Alicia, since he'd always regretted that he had to travel so much for his job and couldn't spend much time with Jordan while she was growing up. Six months later, Ed died of a sudden heart attack. Even though Ed was healthy, I believe that the last two years of his life really took their toll on his poor heart.

Soon after the funeral, Jordan decided to move to another city where a good job was promised to her. She felt she needed to be on her own with Alicia. But I knew that since her father was now gone, Jordan didn't want to stick around with me and unfortunately, I was just too numb with grief to stop her. As it was, I'd never been as close to Jordan as she was to Ed.

After Jordan left I sold our big house and moved into a small, ranch-style home in a nearby suburb. I just hated coming home to that big, old, empty house with all its memories that haunted me night after night. Once I'd settled into my new home, I realized that I would need something to occupy my time, and buying the beauty shop seemed like a great idea. Besides, it was the only skill I knew.

And for the past three years the shop, employees, and customers had kept my loneliness at bay.

Patty was right: The bath relaxed me. Unfortunately, the wine brought back all the memories I was trying so desperately to keep at bay. Then the phone rang loudly, jolting me back to the present.

"Hello?" I answered lazily. The glass of wine had made me drowsy.

"Mom, it's me—Jordan."

"Where are you?" Jordan rarely called me. She'd call on holidays or send me a photo of Alicia and a short letter once in a while. "Are you and Alicia okay?" I asked worriedly.

"Yeah, we're fine." She hesitated. "Mom . . . is it okay if Alicia and I come to visit for a while?"

"Sure, but what about your job?"

She sighed. "I do get vacation time, Mom."

"Of course, you just caught me off guard . . . and half-asleep. I'm just surprised, that's all."

"Well, I just figured that you haven't seen Alicia in a long time and I've been promising her that we'd come to see you."

"Sure; I'd love to see you both! So, when are you coming?"

"Is tomorrow too soon?"

Now, she really had me caught off guard. My small home wasn't set up for company and I had my shop to think about. Still, I didn't want to give Jordan the impression that I didn't want to see her and Alicia. Our relationship had suffered enough over the years.

"No, that's great! But I hope you two can manage while I'm working at the shop."

I jotted down their train number and arrival time. They wouldn't be arriving until early the following evening, so I'd at least have some time to get the house ready. I smiled at the thought of spending time with my granddaughter, whom I'd seen only twice since Jordan moved away.

I checked my watch when I arrived at the train station. I'd lost track of time while preparing things at home and I rushed into the station hoping they hadn't been waiting too long.

I looked up and down the train platform and didn't see them. Then, as I headed for their arrival gate, I spotted them sitting on a bench along the wall.

The sight of them almost broke my heart. They had one battered suitcase between them and they looked like lost souls. My daughter, Jordan, had always been slim, but her faded jeans hung loosely on her hips and Alicia's clothes looked as faded and battered as their suitcase!

My God, how had they been living? Suddenly, I remembered all the times in the past when I'd offered Jordan financial help. She'd always refused. Whenever I brought up money, she always insisted that they were doing just fine. For Christmas and birthdays, at least, I always made sure to send her a generous check in the mail.

Jordan spotted me as I approached and we hugged briefly. "Mom, I almost thought you'd changed your mind!" she said as we drew apart. When I looked at her drawn face I noticed the dark circles under her eyes.

"Now, why would I do that? I'm so happy you came to visit me!"

31

I smiled warmly and looked down at my grandchild's sweet face. I saw Ed in that little girl's face and my eyes misted as I squatted down next to that wide-eyed and quiet little girl. "My goodness, Alicia, you've grown into such a pretty girl! Did you like the train ride?"

Alicia nodded and grinned. She had chestnut hair and a dimpled chin, just like her grandfather. I wished Ed were there to see his lovely little granddaughter as I stood up and Alicia grabbed my hand.

I turned to Jordan as we headed out of the station. "So, how was the train ride?"

"Long!" She sighed. "They must've stopped at every hick town along the way. I'm beat!"

Neither one of us spoke much as I drove along in the light traffic toward home. When I glanced in my rearview mirror, I could see that Alicia had fallen asleep in the backseat, but when I pulled into my driveway a few minutes later, she awoke instantly.

"Is this your house, Grandma?"

I nodded. "Sure is. I guess you don't remember it much. It's been a long time since you've been here." I glanced over at Jordan and she rolled her eyes at me. "I didn't mean anything by that, Jordan. I was just stating a fact to Alicia."

Alicia ran off to check out the backyard. Jordan started to speak, but instead, grabbed her suitcase from the backseat and headed for the front door.

I sighed. Already, I was wondering how many times I would have to defend myself to Jordan during their visit. Even while her father was still alive, it'd always seemed like I could never say or do anything right as far as Jordan was concerned.

Jordan stood in the front doorway, glancing around the living room appreciatively. "You've really done a lot with the place, Mom." She ran a hand over the antique secretary I used for my desk in the dining area. "I'm glad you kept some of Dad's favorite pieces."

I smiled. "Thanks. I like it, too. It finally feels like home for me." I glanced at my daughter. "It's a big change from that big, old house you grew up in, isn't it?" We were silent for a moment and I wondered if Jordan was still angry with me for selling the large, Victorian home that she grew up in. After Ed died, it was just too much for me to take care of alone.

"Mom, I'm sorry about before—in the car, I mean. I know you didn't mean anything. . . ."

Well, this was a switch! My daughter was actually apologizing to me. I smiled. "I know, Jordan. Let's just forget about it."

I showed Jordan the bedroom she would share with Alicia during their stay. I was glad that I'd kept the large bed from the old house that had been in the spare bedroom.

Alicia bounded into the bedroom. Her face was flushed and her eyes were bright. "Mommy!" she said excitedly. "Grandma has real pretty flowers in her backyard and it's big, too! I even saw a bunny!" Alicia glanced around the room. "Is this our room?" she asked as she climbed up onto the large bed and bounced.

"Sure is! Do you like it?" Jordan asked her.

Suddenly, Alicia stopped bouncing and looked down at the floor with tears in her eyes. Jordan sat down next to her.

"What's the matter, hon, don't you like it?"

Alicia shrugged. "There's no toys here," she said sadly. Alicia looked up at me as big, fat tears rolled down her cheeks. "We couldn't bring my toys on the train," she added, her pink lips pouted in sadness.

Thank God I'd had the sense to prepare for this. "Well, I have a surprise for you, honey! Come with me." I took Alicia's hand and winked at Jordan.

I led them both to the den where I'd gathered some of Jordan's old toys and put them into a big box. Alicia squealed as she rummaged through the Barbie dolls, puzzles, a tea set, and more. The biggest surprise was in the closet. When I brought out the three-story, Victorian dollhouse, Alicia's hazel eyes became as round as saucers.

Jordan knelt on the floor beside her daughter to look inside the dollhouse. "I almost forgot about this dollhouse and how fantastic it is . . . I used to spend hours playing with it," she marveled, her pretty face aglow.

"Mommy, was this yours?" Alicia whispered in awe.

"Yes, Alicia. Your grandfather made this for me when I was a little girl just like you. Look—it even has working lights." Jordan pressed a button behind the dollhouse and the whole house lit up inside like fairy magic.

"Wow!" Alicia squealed in delight and investigated the button her mother had pressed.

We left Alicia to her new toys and went into the kitchen where I made some soup and sandwiches for dinner. After our stomachs were full Alicia went back to her toys and Jordan and I relaxed in the den.

"Thanks for getting all that stuff out for Alicia, Mom. She was so upset about leaving all her toys behind."

I waved her words away dismissively. "Oh, I enjoyed it. It brought back a lot of special memories for me. Anyway, maybe you could send for Alicia's things. . . ."

"It's not worth the trouble, Mom. Besides, we'll only be here for a week or two."

After Alicia was in bed for the night, I could tell that Jordan was not in a mood to talk. Soon, she was dozing in front of the TV. As I looked at my sleeping daughter's face, I saw my own child trying so hard to be a mature adult. Unfortunately, at twenty-one, she clearly carried the weight of the world on her shoulders. I knew that she was troubled and needed my help and I was so relieved that she'd finally decided to come to me for it. God only knew how she'd managed alone all that time.

Maybe I should've pressed her more to come home, I thought guiltily.

The shop was closed on Mondays so I had all day to spend with Jordan and Alicia. It was such a nice summer day that I went outside to tend to my flowers.

Alicia was right at my heels and curious about everything. I showed her how to pull weeds, cut the dead flowers away, and water properly. We even peeked in on the young family of rabbits that lived under a large bush at the corner of my yard. I could tell that Alicia enjoyed gardening. Every once in a while she would turn to me, grinning, with dirt smudged all over her cherubic face. I hugged my little granddaughter and laughed.

"Alicia, do you and Mommy have flowers at your house?" I asked.

She frowned. "No. We don't even have a backyard. Mommy says flowers would get trampled at the front of our building so we never planted any."

"That's too bad. So, where do you go to play?" I knew it was wrong, but if Jordan wouldn't tell me anything about her life, I figured I'd find out some things from Alicia.

"Sometimes we go to the park. Mostly I just play in my room."

"Do you have other children to play with?"

"Only when I go to Lucy's house. She has lots of kids to play with at her house."

"Who is Lucy?"

"One of my babysitters. I like Lucy's house best. I always have fun there."

Her answers began to tug at my heart. "So, you have lots of babysitters, huh?"

Alicia nodded.

"Does Mommy have to work a lot?"

"She has two jobs!"

"Two jobs!" I feigned shock. "Wow, Mommy works hard, doesn't she?"

Alicia hesitated. "I like it better now. I like it when Mommy doesn't go to work."

I hugged my granddaughter. "I know you do, honey. That's why you're both here with me—to be together and spend some time with me."

34

Alicia smiled shyly, breaking away from my hug, and went back to her weeding. It brought tears to my eyes to imagine Alicia's life like that—being shuffled from one babysitter to another so her mother could work to put food on their table. A child so young living with all that uncertainty and change. . . .

Jordan had never told me much about their lives. I'd always assumed that she had a forty-hour, weekly office job and had good daycare for Alicia. At least, that was the picture that Jordan had always painted for me. I realized now, though, that I would have to confront her soon if I ever wanted to know the truth.

"Mom?"

I jumped as I shielded my eyes from the sun to look up at Jordan, who was standing over me. She smiled as she watched Alicia play in the dirt.

"She really loves flowers, huh?"

I chuckled. "I guess you can blame that on me. She's got a budding green thumb!"

Jordan hesitated. "Well, I was going to take her to the mall for a bit, but. . . ."

We both smiled at the muddy little girl who played happily at my feet. "Why don't you just leave her here with me? I'm sure you could use a break."

"Really? Are you sure, Mom? I mean, it sure would be nice to shop alone for a change."

"Go. Enjoy yourself. I'm sure she'll be ready for a nap soon, anyway."

Alicia was sorry when we finally had to end our afternoon outside, but I promised her that she could help me with dinner after her nap. As it was, I'd forgotten how active a four-year-old can be! Alicia was such a curious child that I had to keep reasons, answers, and explanations handy at all times!

Jordan was in a good mood when we all sat down to dinner that night. She hummed as she served Alicia her salad and poured her a nice, cold glass of milk.

"Mom, I forgot to tell you that I ran into Tracy at the mall."

I screwed up my face, trying to remember who Tracy was.

Jordan laughed. "You look just like Alicia when you do that. Anyway, I hung out with her for a while back in high school and she's having a few friends over tonight and she wants me to come over."

"Well, that might be nice for Alicia to meet some of your friends. . . ." I began.

"I don't wanna go!" Alicia barked suddenly. "I wanna stay with Grandma!"

Jordan looked at me pleadingly. "Would you mind terribly,

Mom? Besides, there won't be any kids there for her to play with and she'd only be bored."

I shrugged, realizing she had a point. "Okay, then. Alicia stays home with me."

Jordan smiled gratefully.

"Yay!" Alicia yelped. "Grandma can read me a story, right, Grandma?"

"Thanks, Mom," Jordan said, giving me a hug. She helped me clear the table and then rushed to find something to wear for her big night out.

Jordan looked so happy that night that I couldn't disappoint her. However, in the week that followed, she went out every night with Tracy and her friends. I worked at the salon all day and when I came home in the evening, Jordan would leave almost immediately for a night out of drinking, dancing, and socializing. Alicia and I would spend the evening alone.

On Friday afternoon I called home to let Jordan know that I'd have to stay at the shop late that night and close up. Alicia answered the phone when I called.

"This is Grandma, honey. Is Mommy around?"

"She's sleeping, Grandma."

"It's past noon and she's still asleep? Is she sick, pumpkin?"

"She says she's tired and she has a headache."

I could just bet she had a headache! I'd heard Jordan stumble in at three in the morning the night before and it wasn't the first time, either.

"Alicia, go and wake Mommy up. It's very important that I speak with her."

"Okay."

Alicia laid the phone down noisily and I waited for what seemed like forever. Finally, Jordan picked up the receiver.

"Mom, what's wrong?" she asked groggily.

"What's wrong?" I almost screamed. "It's past noon! Shouldn't you be up by now? Has Alicia been roaming the house alone all morning long?"

Jordan sighed loudly. "Mom, Alicia is used to it. She takes care of herself in the mornings."

"That's not the point, Jordan! The point is, I thought you came here to spend time with her—quality time with her—and you haven't been home one evening this week! I don't mind you going out once or twice a week, but every single night. . . ." I glanced toward the front of the shop to make sure the girls hadn't returned from lunch yet.

"I deserve some fun, too, Mom! And Alicia is being well taken care of!"

Yeah—by me, I thought acidly. But I didn't want to argue with Jordan. As it was, I was honestly worried that she might just pick up and leave without even so much as a good-bye and then I knew I wouldn't see Alicia for another two years.

I sighed heavily. "Look—I just wanted to let you know that I have to close up the shop tonight."

"But I made plans with Tracy! It's Friday night, Mom. What will I do with Alicia?"

I tried not to let my voice reveal how angry I was. "Some people have to work, Jordan. I do have a beauty shop to run, you know. Why don't you cancel for tonight and stay home?"

"I can't cancel. Tracy went through a lot of trouble for these concert tickets."

I started to speak, but Jordan cut me off.

"Look, Mom—I'll figure something out. Don't worry about it."

My mouth had just started to open again when I heard the receiver click in my ear. Instantly, I was fuming! Did she think I was her built-in babysitter? I loved Alicia with all my heart, but as her mother, Jordan had a responsibility to her. And did she have to go out every night? I could feel a headache coming on as I rubbed my temples. I felt like I was dealing with a sixteen-year-old all over again. I was too old for this!

As soon as the last customer was out the door I hurriedly closed up the shop and rushed home. I knew as I unlocked the door that the house was empty. Then I spotted the large note taped to the fridge, telling me that Jordan had taken Alicia along with her and not to wait up. Later that night, as I watched the news, the phone rang.

"Hello?"

"Hi, is this Connie Davidson, Jordan's mother?"

"Yes, who is this?"

"You don't know me. My name is Lisa and I'm babysitting for your granddaughter, Alicia. Jordan left me your number in case I had a problem. . . ."

"What's wrong? Is Alicia okay?"

"Well, everything was fine for a while. Alicia was happy playing with my nine-month old, but once I put the baby to bed she started crying and she hasn't stopped. I've tried everything I know to calm her down, but she just keeps insisting that she wants to go home. I just don't know what to do anymore. . . ."

"Let me talk to Alicia."

I heard the phone clatter as Alicia picked it up. She was sniffling loudly.

"It's Grandma, honey. What's the matter?"

"Grandma, I—I want to come home!"

"Don't you like the babysitter, precious?"

"I don't want a babysitter! I want to be with you and Mommy!" She was crying loudly.

"Alicia? I will come and pick you up, but you must stop crying like that this instant. Do you understand?"

She stopped crying, "You promise? Will you come right away?" she hiccuped.

"I promise. Now, put Lisa on the phone so I can get her address."

Thankfully, Lisa lived in a neighboring suburb and I was at her home in ten minutes. Alicia was so happy to see me that she practically knocked me off my feet. I apologized to Lisa and took Alicia home. The poor thing was so exhausted that she fell asleep as soon as we got into the car.

Back at home, I paced the living room after I'd carried Alicia into the house and put her to bed. How could Jordan have left her with a stranger? I couldn't wait to give her a piece of my mind! Lisa had certainly seemed nice enough, but she was still a stranger to Alicia, nonetheless.

Later that night, I heard the key in the door, but didn't have the energy to confront Jordan. There would be time enough for that over the weekend.

Saturday is our busiest day at the shop. I was glad to be busy; it gave me an excuse for sidestepping Patty's questions about the past week at home.

I arrived home that evening and the house was empty, but I could hear music playing in the backyard. I stepped out onto the patio where Jordan was reading a magazine, drinking iced tea, and listening to the radio.

I looked around the yard. "Where's Alicia?"

Jordan removed her sunglasses. "A neighbor invited her over to play with her little girl."

"What neighbor?" I asked, gritting my teeth.

Jordan shot me a dirty look, rolling her eyes as she sipped her iced tea. "Jeez, Mom! Her name is Sara or Sally or something. She lives two doors down and she has a little girl Alicia's age."

I could remember seeing them outside, but I'd never really attempted to make friends with any of my neighbors. I was usually too busy with the shop and all. Still, when I looked over at my neighbor's yard, sure enough, I could see and hear the girls giggling and splashing around in a kiddy pool.

Jordan glanced up at me before returning to her magazine. "See? She's fine."

Silently, I sighed in relief and sat down heavily on a lawn chair next to Jordan. I supposed I had overreacted. We sat in silence for a moment, listening to the girls play two yards over. Then I glanced over at Jordan and she was shaking her head at me.

"I know what you've been thinking, Mom. That I'm not a very good mother."

"I've never thought that, Jordan. I give you a lot of credit for raising a child alone."

Jordan sighed. "I get so tired of being a mother and all the responsibilities that go with it. I love Alicia, but I just don't know if I can handle it alone anymore. . . . ."

"I'm here for both of you. I can always help, Jordan, but I can't be Alicia's mother. She needs you."

Tears welled up in Jordan's eyes. "It's so hard, living in Chicago alone. I have to work a lot of hours just to support us. Poor Alicia has so many babysitters and I'm hardly ever home. . . . ."

"I know. Alicia told me."

Jordan's eyes widened. Then she looked almost angry. "Did she also tell you that I tried the 9-to-5 routine, with a good daycare? But with my lack of skills, I just couldn't make much money. By the time I paid for daycare and paid the rent, I didn't have enough left over for food or clothes. Waitressing has been the only answer." A tear slid down her cheek. "I do the best I can, Mom."

"I know that, Jordan. But why haven't you called me for help? I could've helped you financially and—"

"You and Dad have already done so much for us. How long can I depend on my parents to help me raise my child? I wanted to do it on my own, Mom!" she wailed. "But I failed, didn't I? I mean, here I am—crawling back to you."

I was silent for a moment. "Just because you need help doesn't mean you're a failure, Jordan. Anyone else would've thrown in the towel, but you hung in there. Honey, you must be doing something right. Just look at that smart and beautiful little girl over there."

"Nice try, Mom. But I know I've really messed things up."

"Jordan, if you need money to go back to Chicago, I can help."

Jordan waved my words away, "There's nothing left for me in Chicago. I lost my job and our apartment."

Poor Jordan. I didn't know what to say. "I'm sorry, Jordan." I saw the worry on her face. "Don't worry, honey; we'll figure something out."

On Sunday I packed a picnic lunch and the three of us spent the day at the lake. As we fed the ducks and played ball with Alicia, it reminded me of the days when Ed and I had brought Jordan there. The lake was our favorite place for many years.

Monday, I decided to go to the salon and check my inventory for the upcoming month. I'd gotten so sidetracked by Jordan's visit that

I'd neglected the inventory. Since the shop was closed, I decided to take Alicia along. As it was, I'd been promising to show her the shop. That morning, she was helping me fold clean, warm towels fresh from the dryer when a young man walked into the salon.

I poked my head out from the back room. "Sorry, but we're closed." I went out to meet him with Alicia following behind me.

"Oh, I'm not here for—"

"Hi, Gary! Are you here to see Mommy?" Alicia beamed at the handsome young man as he leaned down and tousled her hair playfully.

"Hey, kiddo!" He glanced toward the back room. "Is Mommy here with you?"

I looked from Alicia to the young man. "Would someone mind introducing us?" I smiled.

The young man stuck out his hand and we shook. "I'm sorry— I'm Gary Statler. Your daughter, Jordan, and I are, uh—friends. You must be Jordan's mom?"

I nodded, smiling. "So, you know Jordan and Alicia from Chicago?"

He nodded. "I'm in town on business for a few days and I wanted to see Jordan, but I didn't have your address. Fortunately, she told me you had a beauty shop, so I looked you up in the phonebook." He shrugged. "I hope you don't mind, but I'd really like to see Jordan."

"Well, why don't we call her, then?"

He seemed like a nice enough young man, but I didn't know him and I didn't know how well Jordan knew him. I called home and the phone rang and rang, but there was no answer. Finally, Gary scribbled a phone number onto a piece of paper and handed it to me.

"Please tell Jordan that I really want to talk to her?"

I nodded as Alicia followed Gary to the front door. "Gary, are you coming back?" she asked him winsomely.

"I hope so, Alicia." He bent down and kissed her cheek. "When I do come back, I'll bring you a present, okay?" She was grinning as Gary waved good-bye through the front window.

I turned to Alicia. "He's a nice man and you like him, don't you?"

"Uh-huh. He took me and Mommy to the park and the beach and lots of times he took us for ice cream. Oh, he brought me presents, too."

This sounds like much more than just a platonic friendship, I mused as I finished folding the towels with Alicia. As usual, Jordan was hiding the truth from me once more. Why? Then that evening at home when I told Jordan about Gary's visit, I was surprised by her reaction.

"You didn't give him our address, did you?"

"Of course not. But, why not? Don't you want to see him? Isn't he a friend of yours as he claims?"

"He used to be, but not anymore! I don't want to see him!" she added firmly.

I hesitated. "He was more than a friend, wasn't he?"

Immediately, Jordan got angry. "It's over, Mom! I don't want to talk about it!"

On that note, she stomped out of the kitchen and moments later I heard her bedroom door slam.

The next day it rained and business was slow. Right before closing time, Gary walked in and I noticed the girls turning their heads to stare at him. I smiled to myself, knowing he'd come back. Patty nudged me with a silly grin on her face when Gary approached the receptionist and asked for me.

"Are you keeping secrets from me?"

I rolled my eyes.

"Who is that hunk?"

"A friend of Jordan's."

She sighed. "Too bad. The best ones are always taken."

I met Gary at the reception desk and introduced him to the girls so they'd stop ogling him.

"I'm sorry to bother you again, but did you give Jordan my message?"

I nodded and his face fell.

"She never called me," he said sadly.

"Gary, maybe you should explain some things to me. Jordan won't tell me much about your, uh . . . relationship."

Gary hesitated.

"I only want to help," I added hopefully.

He looked relieved and then went on to explain that he and Jordan had been dating seriously for the last year. They'd had a big fight over his job transfer and hadn't spoken to each other for a week afterward. Then when he finally called her apartment to apologize, she'd already moved out. Now Gary's company was suddenly transferring him to Atlanta and he didn't want to move without seeing Jordan first. I could sense the urgency in his voice so I picked up the phone and dialed home and Jordan answered.

"Jordan? Gary is here and he wants to talk to you."

"He's at the shop? Mom, I told you I don't want to talk to him!"

Gary took the phone out of my hand. "Jordan, please? I won't be here long. We need to talk. I—"

Gary handed the receiver back to me. Jordan had hung up on him.

"I'm sorry, Gary. My daughter is confused right now. She's

41

trying to sort out her life." I didn't know what else to say to him, but I could see his pain clearly.

He nodded. "I know that. I could help her if she'd let me."

For a moment we were silent. Then, with determination in his voice, Gary turned to me.

"I'll figure out a way; Jordan will talk to me before I go to Atlanta. Thank you for your help, Mrs. Davidson."

I almost applauded him as he left the shop. I knew I'd be seeing him again.

Shortly after, I closed up the shop and rushed home, hoping to convince Jordan to speak to Gary. When I got home I found a note from her taped to the fridge telling me to pick up Alicia at the neighbor's house. Jordan was going out. It looked like Alicia and I would spend another evening alone.

The following morning Alicia and I were eating oatmeal at the kitchen table alone. I didn't have to be at the shop until later that day.

"Maybe your mommy would like some eggs and toast," I suggested to Alicia.

She shrugged with a mouthful of oatmeal. "Mommy's not home."

I rushed into their bedroom and didn't see any of Jordan's clothing strewn about like there usually was after her nights out. Now what? Where was that daughter of mine?

Maybe she spent the night at Tracy's.

I searched the dresser and the nightstand and finally found Tracy's number scribbled on a piece of paper. I called Tracy and she swore to me that she hadn't seen Jordan in a few days. Besides, Tracy had been out of town.

Finally, I spotted the note: Dear Mom, I'm spending a few days with a friend. I'm sorry, but I need to think. Don't worry.

Great! Now, what would I do? I called the shop and explained things to Patty and she said, "Just bring Alicia with you. We won't be that busy today and she'll be fine."

I quickly packed a few of Alicia's toys into a plastic shopping bag and she did seem happy about spending the day at the shop. The girls adored her and the day ran smoothly, after all.

After three days, though, the routine was tiring for Alicia and me. It was the end of the week and Jordan still hadn't called. I was beside myself with worry.

What on earth was I supposed to do? Did Jordan actually think that leaving her daughter behind with just a note to explain her whereabouts was acceptable behavior? Had she really just up and left her? I was furious and worried. And then the realization hit me:

My daughter had abandoned her child!

By Saturday, Alicia was bored with the shop. We were so busy that day that I had to confine her to the back room. I felt like I was holding the poor child prisoner, but it was for her own safety. Even then, I already knew that I couldn't just keep dragging Alicia to the shop with me. I prayed that Jordan would be back before the new week started.

Alicia was in a somber mood on Monday and when I suggested that we go to our favorite park by the lake, she finally broke down and cried. Fat tears welled up in her eyes and rolled down her plump little cheeks.

"What's the matter, honey?" I held out my arms to her and Alicia rushed to me and wept.

"Where's my mommy? Why didn't she say good-bye to me? Why doesn't she come back?" she blubbered, and I grabbed a tissue and told her to blow her nose.

"Well, everything just happened so fast, honey. Your mommy is trying to find a job and find you both a nice place to live," I lied, desperate to comfort her.

"But I don't want to move! I like it here with you!" Alicia wailed.

"I know you do, honey, and I love having you here."

She sniffled loudly. "What if Mommy doesn't ever come back?"

"Oh, but, honey—of course she will! She loves you very much and she'll come back soon. You'll see." I patted her cheek, smiled reassuringly, and then told her to get her ball to take to the park.

With Patty's help I managed to stay at home with Alicia for most of that following week. In the meantime, I made arrangements with my neighbor, Sara, to have her watch Alicia for me later that week. At least I knew now that with Sara, Alicia would be well taken care of and have a playmate at the same time. I didn't want to think any farther ahead than that week. Deep down, I didn't want to believe that Jordan could abandon her own child.

It was Sunday, ten days after Jordan had left. Alicia was playing in Sara's backyard. I was tending to my flowerbed when the phone rang. I ran inside to pick it up.

"Mom?"

I was so relieved and yet, I was also very angry the minute I heard Jordan's voice. Everything tumbled out of me all at once.

"Where are you? We've been so worried! Why didn't you call sooner?"

"It's hard to explain, Mom. I know you must be angry, but I can't talk long. I'm on a payphone."

"Jordan, you have to come home! Right now. Alicia thinks you've deserted her and I'm beginning to wonder myself!"

"Didn't you read my note?"

"A note is not good enough, Jordan! Besides, you've been gone more than a few days. Now, when are you coming home?" I asked angrily.

She hesitated. "I don't know, Mom."

I tried to calm myself, gritting my teeth at her answer. "Jordan, I know that you have problems and I told you that we would work them out together, but running away won't solve anything."

Jordan's voice began to quiver. "You don't understand, Mom."

"You're right, Jordan! I don't understand! Because you don't tell me anything! Alicia wants you home and so do I. We can talk about things when you come home." I could sense her hesitation over the phone. Then I had an idea that I thought might work. "Look, Jordan—I'll give you a few more days and then, if you don't come home, I am calling Children's Welfare!"

"Mom, you wouldn't!"

"Would you like to bet your daughter's future on that?"

Jordan was silent for a moment and I pleaded with her once more to come home. But my words fell on deaf ears. Finally, Jordan spoke.

"Tell Alicia that I love her. Good-bye Mom."

She hung up before I could say another word.

I had been harsh and the threat of calling Children's Welfare probably didn't help matters one bit. But I was getting desperate. All of a sudden, all those feelings I had as a mother back when Jordan was a teenager washed over me all over again—the desperation her father and I felt, the guilt, anger, and hopelessness of raising a troubled teen. I knew then that for Alicia's sake, I could never call Children's Welfare. If Jordan couldn't—or wouldn't—care for her, then Alicia would stay with me, forever if necessary.

The following night I heard the key in the door and I knew it was Jordan. I gave her a few moments and then joined her in the kitchen.

She looked terrible! Her clothes were all wrinkled, her eyes were bloodshot, and her straight hair hung limply on her shoulders. When our eyes met she burst into tears. I pulled my chair next to hers and put my arm around her shoulders.

"I'm sorry, Mom. I just—I didn't know what to do! Oh, Mom—I'm so confused!" she wailed.

"Jordan, if it's a matter of money, you're both welcome to stay here for as long as you want. You could find a job and a good sitter for Alicia. School will be starting soon and she really seems to like it here. . . ." I hesitated and then smiled. "Maybe you could both like it here?" I searched Jordan's tearstained face. "Please, Jordan, let me help?"

She grabbed a napkin from the lazy Susan on the table and wiped her tears. "It's not that, Mom. . . ."

I started to speak—and then it hit me. "Then, what is it?"

Strangely, as I looked at Jordan and waited for an answer, a familiar feeling from the past overwhelmed me. I almost placed my hands over my ears, knowing the answer before she said it.

"I'm pregnant!" my daughter blurted out.

"What?"

My mouth hung open. Again? I wanted to faint at those words. And then suddenly, I knew: Gary. It must be Gary! I finally forced myself to speak.

"It's Gary's baby, isn't it? He's the father, isn't he?" I held my breath.

Jordan nodded, fresh tears coming at her admission. "He doesn't know and I refuse to beg another man to take care of a child he doesn't want!"

"But, Jordan—Gary has a right to know!"

"Why?" She stared at me angrily. "So he can run out on me, too?"

"Jordan, I know that you're bitter about Alicia's father, but Gary is not a teenager. He seems like an honest, decent young man. I happen to like him and so does Alicia. Are you even thinking of her? She needs a father, Jordan. Telling Gary that you're pregnant with his child is not entrapment or a life sentence to all men! Obviously, he has some feelings for you or he wouldn't have traveled all this way and shown up on my doorstep, begging to see you."

Jordan was silent for a moment. Shaking her head, she said, "I can't believe I almost went through with it."

"Went through with what?" But I knew the answer and I clamped my hands over my mouth as the realization hit me of why she'd run off.

She looked up at me, her face pale and drawn. "I almost did it, Mom. I was that close to having an abortion. I just didn't want to raise another child alone." The tears started down her face again. "I love Gary, but I don't want him to feel trapped, and God knows it would be a lot for him to handle—an instant family. . . ."

"From what I've seen of Gary, I don't think he would ever feel trapped, Jordan."

She hesitated. "I . . . I just need a little more time, and then I'll call him."

Finally, we agreed on something. I wouldn't push her; I was just glad to have my daughter home safe, problems and all. Alicia needed her mother no matter what.

The following day Gary came to the shop. "Well, Mrs. Davidson, it's final. I leave for Atlanta in a few days. I've already taken care of my belongings and my apartment back in Chicago." In desperation, he added, "I really need to see Jordan, Mrs. Davidson. I just can't leave without seeing her."

45

Little did Gary know that I had already formulated a plan for him to see Jordan. I explained to him then that I would go home and send Jordan back to the shop to get some important bookkeeping work that I had to get done over the weekend.

Gary thought it just might work and hugged me in appreciation. "You won't regret this, Mrs. Davidson," he said, grinning happily. "I promise!"

My plan worked and that night, Jordan and Gary came home together and I could see the happiness in their faces. Gary was thrilled about the pregnancy and they would soon be married.

I suggested to them that Alicia stay with me while they headed on to Atlanta to do some house hunting and plan their little wedding celebration. Besides, it was a good excuse for me to spend some more time with my beautiful granddaughter. As it was, I'd become so accustomed to having her around that I already knew my heart would ache once she was gone. Alicia took me back in time to the days when Jordan was small and Ed was alive and we were all so happy.

A few weeks later, I escorted Alicia to Atlanta to join her mom and new dad. Alicia was happy and excited, especially since she'd have her own house, bedroom, and a yard to play in. Jordan and Gary had rented a three-bedroom house in a nice suburb outside the city. As Jordan and I walked the streets of the quaint neighborhood, I noticed all the bicycles, toys, and swing sets in the yards. A few young mothers were outside, chatting as their children played.

I smiled and nodded at the sight. "You were right, Jordan—this is a perfect neighborhood for a young family."

This was what I had wanted for Jordan all along. I guess some dreams just take a little longer to materialize.

I returned to Indianapolis and my beauty shop, alone. I knew I would have to get used to being alone all over again. I would miss my granddaughter's giggling and her nonstop chatter as we worked side by side in my garden.

Six months later, Jordan gave birth to a healthy baby boy. It brought tears to my eyes when Jordan told me that they'd named my new grandson after Ed. I knew it would make him so proud.

Then in November of that same year, I tore open a letter from Jordan and an airline ticket fell out and floated to the floor. Jordan and Gary had invited me to spend the holidays with them; after all, I still had not been formally introduced to my new grandson! Besides, I had a very special gift for Alicia.

So I carefully wrapped and packed up Jordan's Victorian dollhouse and all the little pieces of miniature furniture. I sealed it all up tightly in a sturdy box and on the outside, in bold letters, I wrote:

DO NOT OPEN UNTIL CHRISTMAS! I wanted to be there when Alicia opened her gift.

Suddenly, a tear slid down my cheek. I only wish that Ed could be there, too, I thought. I wish he could see how well things have turned out for our daughter, Jordan.

But I did honestly feel that, even though he was in heaven, Ed had somehow been guiding me through all of this all along.

In a recent dream, he told me that I should "rest easy now"—that we both can now be at peace with our daughter and our past.

We must've done something right, after all.

THE END

VIGILANTE GRANNY
A robber won't get the best of me

"Grandma! Grandma! Are you all right?" My fifteen-year-old great-granddaughter, Mackenzie, rushed toward me, looking as if she intended to wrap her arms around my shoulders. She skidded to a halt, a look of apprehension on her face, when she caught sight of the bandage stretching from my wrist to my elbow.

"I'm fine, dear," I assured her, reaching out to take her hand in mine. I gave it a little squeeze, hoping to cheer her some.

"Look at your arm, Grandma! Does it hurt much?" I could see the fear and worry in Mackenzie's eyes and took notice of the quiver in her voice.

"My arm is nearly as good as new. This old wrap is just a preventive measure to protect my arm and make sure that I don't sprain it again."

Mackenzie gasped, and I sensed her distress. I knew she'd fought to keep the tears forming in her eyes from falling. I circled her waist with my good arm and hugged her.

"I told you, dear—I'm fine." I chuckled to lighten the mood, and added, "You should see the other guy, though!"

Mackenzie dropped her head on my shoulder and buried her face. She didn't laugh, and I figured she didn't care much for my sense of humor about such a serious matter. I patted her shoulder.

My son, Scott, joined the conversation. "That's not funny, Mother. You could've been maimed or killed. You had no business confronting that criminal."

Mackenzie shuddered at the mention of the word "killed." I hugged her tighter. Scott's stern comment let me know that he appreciated my humor even less than his granddaughter did, and that he thought of my actions as impulsive. The eldest of my three sons, Scott could be a little bossy at times. His face mirrored his tone as he bestowed on me one of the looks he usually reserved for his children and grandchildren as he verged on reprimanding them.

Now that his "behave yourself" expression presented itself to me, I stifled another chuckle. I couldn't help it, since I found it funny that my son thought that he could intimidate me. It mattered little that he stood before me with his six-foot-frame stretched over a foot above my head—nor did I concern myself with the detail that he would be sixty-four on his next birthday. At any age or size, he remained the son and I the mother. Intimidation didn't work on me. If it did,

Scott and I would not have been embroiled in an emotional verbal exchange about my decision to foil a robbery attempt. Besides the fact I interrupted a theft in progress, Scott harped on the particulars that I'm eighty-five and walk with a cane. That I didn't hesitate to take on the robber even with the odds against me pretty much confirmed that I'm not easily intimidated. I stood my ground and met the defiance in my son's eyes.

"Don't look at me like I've taken leave of my senses, Scott."

"I'm afraid you may have done just that. Whatever possessed you to challenge an armed robber? As it is, you can barely stand on your own two feet."

"I can stand, dear; it's walking that gives me trouble."

Scott sighed, obviously growing tired of my quips, and for the briefest moment, I regretted causing him such anguish.

"Mother, I cannot believe you are treating this situation so lightly. There is nothing funny about it. You thwarted a would-be criminal in the midst of committing a serious offense! Men like him kill innocent people and never give their actions a second thought."

"I understand you're upset, Scott, but everything turned out fine. My humor helps me to keep things in perspective."

Scott shook his head in a slow and deliberate motion and let his breath slip out in a long exhale. "Everything did not turn out fine, and I am not going to pretend it did. Look at your arm, bandaged from top to bottom."

He drew his gaze in a path from my wrist to my elbow. "And your neck and shoulder have bothered you since you were thrown to the ground. You're lucky that bum didn't snap your neck." He ran a hand through his hair, looking exasperated, and said, "I'm also trying to keep things in perspective. I don't want to get a call someday from the police telling me that my mother has fallen victim to some thug."

Mackenzie tightened her hold on me and sniffled. Even though a protest formulated in my head, I decided to keep quiet so my great-granddaughter would be spared further anxiety. After all, I knew it would do little good to argue with Scott when he'd made up his mind about something. He inherited his stubborn streak from me, and had been challenging me since his childhood. We are both of the mindset that we know best and are unlikely to change our opinions even when pressured to do so.

Scott must have taken my silence for compliance, because he continued reciting a string of reasons why I should have minded my own business in the first place—and he knew better than to make the suggestion. I hardly ever minded my business if I thought I could help a person or else fix things in some way. When I let the lecture pass without comment, Scott increased the pressure by adding another tactical move—

playing on my emotions—which he must've known would get a rouse from me. He hit me where he knew that it mattered the most.

"I would think you would want to take care of yourself so that you can be around for your grandchildren and great-grandchildren."

Scott, knowing full well that my grandchildren and great-grandchildren are the lights of my life, had resorted to using them to keep me docile, which I considered a low blow for him. My sons and daughters often admonished me for lavishing affection on their children with blatant disregard for their faults. But I cannot help it; I love them with all my heart. Even so, I couldn't let Scott continue unchecked. I stood my ground, sticking to my lifelong convictions of helping others and doing whatever I could to better my community.

"Scott, you know how deeply I love all the children. It's because I love them so much that I don't want them growing up in a crime-ridden world. I've devoted years to keeping our community corruption-free. And you know full well that your father and I encouraged you and your brothers and sisters to get involved and give back, too. I can't understand why you are making such a fuss. Why do you think I worked all those years with various organizations and served on so many committees?"

Scott countered. "PTA and Chamber of Commerce meetings are a different story from confronting criminals. I hardly think voting on the latest fundraiser could get you killed."

"You think that's what my life's been about? Fundraising? Well, committees I've served on have implemented programs and ordinances to keep crime to a minimum, and have allowed the townspeople to gain some peace of mind. We volunteered our time and labor so that our children and grandchildren could live a better life, and I intend to work for this community as long as I'm a part of it! By the way, those fundraisers provided playgrounds, sports equipment, emergency services, and a wealth of other materials."

"I know, Mother. I apologize for making your efforts seem trivial. I'm aware of your accomplishments. It's your risking life and limb I have a problem with. After all, I want you to be a part of this community for a long time."

I shrugged off his last remark. "I'm not sorry for helping that poor store clerk. She was just a young girl and froze the instant the crook approached her. If I hadn't interceded, he may have beaten or kidnapped her so that she wouldn't be able to identify him. I didn't see anyone else around to help, and I reacted."

Scott shook his head. "That's the problem. I'm disappointed in your lack of judgment."

"I only did what anyone else would do in similar circumstances," I explained.

Scott remained unconvinced, and continued lecturing me on the foolishness of my ways before ending with the remark, "No, Mother. Most people would not risk their lives if they knew they could get hurt or killed. They would be quiet, and hope to get out of the situation in one piece."

I shook my head. Now I was the one disappointed by his response. "No, Scott. You're the one who's wrong. There are people who risk their lives every day to help others. They're the first to arrive on the scene of an accident, they respond to catastrophes and emergencies, and they just pitch in whenever they're needed. This world is full of people who never think of themselves when the time comes to assist others, whether they're friends or strangers. They fight constantly to make this world a secure place for their families and everyone else. It saddens me to think you want me to turn my back on someone facing a hardship. Wouldn't you come to the aid of someone in dire circumstances?"

"Yes, but—"

Scott started to protest, but I could not endure further lecturing from him and raised my hand, silencing his next words. "I'm tired. I need to lie down for a while."

Scott sighed, but he quieted.

"I'll help you to your room, Grandma." Mackenzie's voice cut through the tension and cold words that had been spoken, relieving me of a continuation of the reprimand.

"Thank you, dear."

Later, alone in my room, I pondered Scott's words and assessed them in relation to my principles. I'm sure some people would run from adversity and avoid putting themselves in jeopardy to save others, as Scott suggested. Luckily, I believe as many people will roll up their sleeves and pitch in when needed. I've always been the latter type of person. When I see something that needs to be done, I ask myself: Who will do this if I don't do it?

My answer is always the same. I do it.

Ever since I could remember, I loved my town and the people in it. I'd spent my entire life in the same neighborhood—a protected, close-knit community. I attended grade school, junior high, and high school surrounded by friends and neighbors who were like an extended family to me. I jumped rope in the streets with my friends, played hide-and-seek after dark, and walked to the corner candy store without fear. It didn't matter what time of day or night we roamed. We didn't worry about kidnappers, child predators, drug lords, and murderers. We didn't have carjackings, drive-by shootings, and villains brazenly attempting to hold up banks and convenience stores. Adults and children could go anywhere in town without fear.

Neighbors looked out for one another, and made it their business to check on all the children and elderly in town. We all lazed away the hours in conversations on porches or over backyard fences. Summertime brought street fairs, dances, and neighborhood block parties. Holidays were made extra special with all the traditional and non-traditional celebrations, church services, foods, and gifts. At Halloween, witches and ghosts decorated porches everywhere while trick-or-treaters went from house to house. For every holiday and occasion, our town was safe, peaceful, and fun.

Caleb, the man I married, lived next door to my grandparents. Over the years we became childhood playmates, friends, and eventually, a couple. During high school Caleb worked part-time at the local factory, and the job turned into full-time after he graduated. I took an office job at the local hospital when I finished high school.

Caleb and I became engaged graduation night and saved for our wedding, which we planned for the following June. I remember my mother telling me, "We are so glad you chose to marry Caleb. He comes from an honest, hard-working family. He will be a wonderful provider and a good husband."

"I know, Mom. He's the one for me."

Caleb and I married in the church where we were both baptized and had a small reception in the church hall. Both of our families had been friends for many years, and they were thrilled with our marriage.

Caleb's paycheck allowed us to rent a tiny two-bedroom house near his parents' home, and my salary went toward saving for a place of our own. Two years into our marriage, we bought our first home. Shortly after we moved in, I gave birth to our son, Scott. As was typical of the forties, men worked while their wives cared for the homes and children. I quit my job at the hospital and filled my days with caring for Scott, Caleb, and our home. Time passed happily.

Women in the community baby-sat one another's children, shared recipes and baked goods, tended flower gardens, and canned vegetables and fruits. We all took pride in keeping an eye out for strangers in our community in order to keep corruption away from our children and us. We lived a relatively peaceful existence.

My little family's tranquility ended, as did that of the entire nation, when World War II began. Caleb went overseas to fight, and I wrote letters, worried daily, and kept our home in order until he returned, which, thankfully, he did. During Caleb's absence, Scott must have asked me a hundred times, "Where's Daddy? When is he coming home?"

Each time, I would answer, "Daddy loves you so much that he went far away to make the world a better place."

"But I don't want Daddy to go away," Scott whined.

My reply was always the same. "I know, honey. I miss him, too. He'll be home as soon as he can." Scott and I prayed nightly for Caleb's return; he came back to us without injury.

Our lives settled once more into a routine, but Caleb came home a changed man. He appreciated his life, and us, more intensely. He reminded Scott on a daily basis how fortunate he was to live in this great country, and he encouraged me to never take my family and life for granted.

Sunday church services became especially meaningful in our efforts to count our blessings and offer thanks. Caleb also became active in local events and worked with lawmakers when policies affecting our hometown were introduced and voted into law. As Caleb's involvement in community affairs grew, so did mine. I joined the PTA and volunteered at the church and in our local representative's office. I organized school and political fundraisers and became an advocate of social responsibility.

In time, Caleb and I bought a larger house, and our family grew by two additional sons and two daughters. It seemed that in no time at all, Scott entered high school.

Caleb and I raised our children to participate in their community, and our family became well regarded in town. We didn't care how they chose to become involved; we merely encouraged the children to be concerned citizens and responsible adults. Therefore, in addition to Caleb's and my contributions, our sons and daughters volunteered in the hospital, the fire department, girl scouts, and the church.

Unfortunately, Caleb never lived long enough to see the successes of his children come to fruition. He died six months before our youngest son's graduation. One of our daughters was in grade school at the time, the other, in junior high.

As usual in our supportive town, neighbors were wonderful during that dark time. They brought food, kept the children and me company, and cried with us. These good people did not forget us once the funeral was over as so often happens. They continued to drop by with baked goods and casseroles. A couple of the men, who were Caleb's close friends, made minor house repairs and kept my old car running while my own sons were off getting their college educations through scholarships they'd received.

After Scott graduated from college, he came back home to live so he could help me take care of the house and his younger brother and sisters. My son, Kip, graduated college a year after Scott, and he moved to California and took a job in a large company.

The other children eventually grew up, finished college, and married. One of my daughters moved to Darien; the other bought a house a block from mine. My youngest son lived in town until his death at the age of twenty-five from a car accident. Scott married his high school sweetheart, as I had done, and he moved his new wife into the bedroom he occupied in my home. To this day I share my house with Scott and his wife. His grown children, who also grew up in my house, married and live nearby with my great-grandchildren.

Although walking is difficult for me, I continue to do what I can for my community and to help around the house. I manage pretty well with a cane and am thankful that I have wonderful friends to give me a hand whenever I need it. My friend, Jill, is one of those angels who help me get where I need to go. She drove me to the store the day of the incident with the robber.

My social security check had arrived that Wednesday morning, and Jill offered me a ride to the bank and a local variety store. She pulled up to the front curb at the variety store and came around to open my door.

"Here's your cane, Myra. I'm going to park the car, and I'll meet you at the candy counter just inside the door. I'll grab a shopping cart on my way in so you can lean on it while shopping, instead of using your cane."

Jill was such a dear!

I stood near the counter and watched the young lady fill the cases with fresh chocolates. I love chocolate, and easily became engrossed in watching the cases fill with the tempting delights. I was not distracted so much that I missed the young man come up on the far side of the counter, however. He approached the clerk and demanded, "Give me all your money."

The clerk seemed frozen in place until the man pulled something from his jacket pocket and waved his hands wildly toward the cash register, shouting in a louder voice. Without giving it much thought, I went behind him and hit him on the head with my cane as hard as I could, hoping to knock some sense in his head. When he turned around, I realized he towered above me. I raised my cane higher and yelled, "You want money? Go get a job and leave this girl alone!" And I walloped him again.

The man shoved me out of the way and ran out the door. I fell down and my cane went sprawling, but luckily Jill showed up then and got me back together. The clerk ran over to help, too. Fear lingered in her eyes. I read her nametag—Lena.

"We're going to be fine, Lena," I assured her. "That terrible man is gone, and I'm sure he won't be coming back any time soon. You go call 911 and tell the police to come here."

Lena cried and hugged me. "You are so wonderful. I don't know what I would have done had I been alone. You stayed calm and took control. You're a guardian angel!"

54

She called 911, and when the police arrived, an officer approached me. "Do you remember what he looked like? Can you give me a description?"

"Sure, I can give you a description," I said. "He wasn't very bright, if you ask me. He didn't have his face covered or anything. Imagine how thoughtless—robbing a store and not using a disguise."

"That's an advantage for us. Let's start from the beginning. Think carefully, now. I need to know everything you remember. No detail is too small."

"I recall standing over there by the wall. I had myself propped against it and waited for Jill to bring me a shopping cart. It's easier for me to get around the store with a cart."

"I understand, Mrs. Higgins. What time was that?"

"I guess around ten-thirty. Jill picked me up at ten, and it doesn't take that long to get over to the store."

"Okay. You were standing against the wall. Then what happened?" the officer asked.

"A young man came in and walked over to the counter. He didn't see me. Don't think he even bothered to look around the store."

The officer scribbled in his notebook. "He was alone?"

"Yes."

"How about his clothing? Can you remember what he wore?"

"He had on a pair of jeans and a navy blue sweatshirt."

"Did he wear glasses or have any distinguishable marks that you noticed?"

"No glasses. No marks I noticed. He was tall—at least as tall as Scott."

The officer shook his head. He knew Scott. Most people in town did.

"So he came in the front door and walked to the counter, right? Did you see the weapon?"

"He came in the front door, but I didn't see a weapon. He stood close to the edge of the counter and leaned toward the clerk. At first, I thought he wanted to ask her about some merchandise. Then I heard him tell her to open the cash register and give him all the money in it. He sort of slurred his words."

"And what did Lena, the clerk, do at that point?"

"She didn't move. Too frightened, I guess. Then he reached into his pocket and pulled something out. I didn't get a good look at what he had right then."

"Ah, huh. But you thought he had a weapon?"

"He started shouting in a mean, rough voice, 'I'll smash your hand and break every one of your fingers if you don't open that register now.' Then he slammed something down on the counter to make his point and yelled, 'Do it!'"

55

The officer looked sympathetic and said, "I'm sure he frightened both of you."

I shook my head in agreement. "I can tell you my heart pounded like crazy. I felt sorry for the poor saleswoman, though. From where I stood, I could see her hands shaking something awful, and she looked ready to burst into tears at any moment. I scanned the store, hoping to spot another customer, but no one else was in the store. I couldn't stand by and do nothing, so I decided to take matters in my own hands at that point and sneaked up behind him. By the time he got the last words out to Lena, I began hitting him over the head with my cane as hard as I could. He ducked and shielded his head with his arm, but I kept hitting him again and again until he turned around."

The officer flipped the page in his notebook and chuckled. "Huh? You did what? Pretty feisty, aren't you? What happened when the suspect turned around and saw you?"

"He looked me in the eyes, but there was no malice in his. He had a dumb expression on his face, like nothing registered. Then he shoved me aside and ran out the door. I fell over and my cane slid out of my reach. Jill showed up and Lena ran over to help me. She kissed my cheek and called me her guardian angel. I'm no angel, I just couldn't stand by and let that man rob the store."

"All right, that should do it. Thanks, Mrs. Higgins. Your description will be quite helpful in catching this guy."

The officer turned to Jill and asked for her account of the incident. Jill arrived in time to see the man fleeing the store and to help Lena get me to my feet. After Jill gave her brief report, Lena recounted her version of the attempted robbery. Finally, Jill and I did our shopping. Lena's manager came in the store and thanked me over and over for preventing the robbery and a possible catastrophe. She sent Lena home to recover from her fright.

I'd hoped to forget the incident and get back to normal. I didn't want any publicity, but word spread throughout the neighborhood within hours of a news report on television. The report did not give my name, but I guess the description gave me away. Many of the townspeople called the house with well wishes and congratulations. The local paper caught wind of the story and wanted to interview me. They ran a small article that evening and a much larger one in the weekend edition. For some reason a reporter thought it newsworthy that a woman my age would take on a would-be robber. After the local item appeared in the paper, a larger city paper called and sent someone to interview me. They ran a full-page story with a picture, and newswires nationwide picked up the story. It surprised me how much attention I got, but nothing prepared me for a call from a national talk show. The producer heard my story and wanted me to appear on the show. To me, it seemed like a lot of attention for being a good citizen.

A knock at my bedroom door interrupted my reminiscing, rousing me back to the present. "Come in."

My great-granddaughter entered, looking happier than when I'd seen her earlier in the day. She said, "It's time for dinner, Grandma. Are you coming down to eat?"

I returned her smile and pulled myself up to a sitting position. "Sure. I just need to freshen up a bit before coming down."

Mackenzie plopped down on the edge of my bed. "Did you have a nice nap?"

I laughed. "Actually, I didn't get much sleep. I was thinking about when your grandfather was your age."

Mackenzie wrinkled her nose. "Grandpa? It's hard to image him at my age."

We both laughed. "I'll see you downstairs."

To my chagrin, the topic of conversation at dinner wound its way to the robbery attempt when Scott's wife, Ruby, voiced her opinion.

"You only hurt your arm and shoulder, Mother, but you need to think about other serious injuries you could've sustained. What if you'd broken that bad hip of yours? Your shopping days would've ended once and for all."

"I'm feeling fine now," I said.

"Well, the next time you want to go shopping, Mother, I'll take you—or else Scott will. It's not safe for you to be out alone."

"I was not alone. And I stood up to that thug in the first place to prevent him from bringing crime into this community. I will not be his victim and will shop with my friends whenever they are available to take me."

"Oh, no you won't," a chorus of voices responded.

I stood up, pushed my chin out, and took a deep breath. "If I wouldn't let a thief steal my freedom, I won't let any of you take it, either. I've been going shopping with Jill and my friends for years."

"You're all getting older now, Mother," Scott said.

"Even if I am, having you by my side won't guarantee my safety."

"At least I can stop you from fighting off robbers," he muttered.

I laughed to break the tension. "Can you? Since when could anyone stop me from doing what I want?"

No one else laughed, and I continued.

"I lived in this town when people didn't fear going shopping or anywhere else alone, and that thug won't keep me from living my typical life."

Scott started to protest, but I conceded before he could get carried away. "I know. Things could've gotten out of hand. I'm sorry for worrying you, but I just couldn't let that man get away with terrorizing that young clerk. You know I'm not likely to sit back and mind my own business, but I'll try in the future. Now, who wants pie?"

After dinner, my son, Kip, called. He expressed his concerns for my health and well-being. Although troubled about my lack of good judgment regarding the lawbreaker, Kip understood why I confronted the man. He gave me strict orders, however, to be careful in the future. Then he said he loved me and was proud of me. His comments bolstered my esteem.

Later, while sitting in the living room, my great-grandson, Ryan, burst into the room brandishing the daily newspaper with the article about me. "Hey, everybody, look at this!" He flashed open the paper. "Look! Grandma made the front page."

"Oh, no." I moaned.

"Let me see," Mackenzie said.

"What's it say?"

"It says Grandma is a hero. And she's spirited. What does spirited mean? She's a ghost or something?"

Scott's irritation caused him to snap at his grandson and grab the paper. "No, it doesn't mean your grandmother is a spirit. Let me have that paper." He read without speaking for several minutes.

"Spirited means that I don't take any nonsense, dear," I explained.

"The paper said Grandma's a hero?" Mackenzie echoed Ryan's words.

Scott sighed. "It says the alleged robber threatened the salesclerk with a weapon."

"A weapon!" Mackenzie gasped and wrapped her arms around my neck.

"He had a wrench, dear. That's all," I explained.

"Wow! He could've bashed your head in with it," Ryan added, much to my dismay.

Scott blew out an exaggerated breath. "Ryan is right, and you're lucky the robber didn't do exactly that and more, Mother. The guy is a foot taller than you and over fifty years your junior. I'd say that combination, and a weapon, gives him a decided edge."

I rolled my eyes to the ceiling and gave my head a little shake. "Scott, you are far too cynical. And you're frightening the children with that kind of talk! I had a weapon of my own."

I picked up my cane from where it rested against the side of the couch and raised it a foot or so off the floor. Ryan came over and tapped the cane. "Yeah, that metal would really hurt when you hit someone over the head. How many times did you smash his head, Grandma? Did you give him a lump?"

I couldn't help but laugh at his enthusiasm. "The truth is that I whacked him so hard he couldn't even see straight."

"How many times did you hit him, Grandma?" Ryan asked again.

"I'm not sure; maybe three or four times. I just kept hitting him, hoping to knock some sense into his head! A man his age should have been working, instead of trying to make money the easy way. He admitted to being on drugs, too. Do you children see the crazy things that drugs make you do? Stay away from drugs. They'll ruin your life."

They both said at the same time, "Don't worry, Grandma. We will."

Mackenzie and Ryan went back to reading the newspaper article, and my thoughts drifted to Scott's high school days, when our community experienced an incident that marred our serenity and our security. Several juniors and seniors were rounded up in a drug raid at a local park. Scott worked that night at his part-time job, but when he came home, Caleb and I had a long heart-to-heart talk with him about the dangers of taking drugs.

"Don't ever get mixed up in drugs, son," Caleb advised. "I heard too many horror stories about atrocities linked to drugs while I was overseas, fighting. The problems in this country regarding drugs are just getting started."

Scott assured us he would never take drugs. "I know, Dad. My friends and I talk about the drug problems at school. We know those kids taking them are ruining their health and their lives. You don't have to worry about me."

We believed him. I empathized with my neighbors and friends who had children involved in the episode, however. Caleb and I joined many of them in a citizen's group organized to fight the drug problem and drive it out of our town. The committee worked hard and instituted programs and disseminated information in the schools, which dramatically reduced the drug problem. I shook off the memories and tuned in to the family's discussion about the newspaper article.

"All right. Enough of this talk about robbers! Why don't you children go and read a book? I don't know why my picture and story are in the paper, anyhow. People need to let the whole subject rest. The criminal is in jail. He won't be causing any more trouble for a while. Maybe he'll get his drug problem treated while he's incarcerated. As it is, he apologized for his behavior. Now he'll have additional time to think about his actions. And maybe when he gets out of prison, he'll get himself a job like other people do when they need money."

"I'm going to get a job when I'm old enough," Mackenzie assured me.

"I know you will, dear."

I thought the issue would finally be dropped, but the phone rang. Another neighbor had heard the news and called to get the details. I'd barely hung up the phone when another friend, who had seen the local paper, called to congratulate me. I honesty didn't know why people were making such a fuss. I did what any other concerned citizen would do.

My daughter, Gretchen, her husband, Dave, and their two children came to visit that evening, as did Ellen, my youngest daughter. Ellen lives in Lake Erie. Her family didn't come with her since her trip came up unexpectedly.

"Show them the picture of Grandma in the paper!" Ryan yelled. "Grandma's a hero," he told everyone.

Gretchen ignored his comments and ran over to the couch where I sat. She plopped down and gave me a quick hug.

"Mother! Oh, my goodness—look at you! How is your arm? Does your neck hurt? Are you taking any pain medications?"

Gretchen, who happens to be a registered nurse, picked up my hand and inspected the bandage.

"Who wrapped this thing? I think it's too tight. Your wrist is turning blue."

I assured her the bandage felt fine, but she continued to fret over me for the next half an hour, anyway. Scott, in the meantime, had found an ally in Dave. The two of them recounted the foolishness of taking on an armed robber with a cane. I remind them the armed robber had a "weapon" that didn't shoot bullets.

"Let me see that article," Ellen said, taking the newspaper from Scott. "Where was Jill when all this happened, Mother? I thought she took you shopping?"

"She did take me. She went outside to get me a shopping cart so it would be easier for me to walk around the store."

"It says here he threatened the clerk. Where were you standing? Did you see the wrench?" Ellen asked.

"I stood near the door and didn't see the wrench until he dropped it. Would you all please put that paper away? You're going to give the children nightmares," I complained.

"I don't know why they used your name and picture. What if this character retaliates when he's released from prison?" Ellen asked.

Scott broke into the conversation. "The first report in the paper didn't print her name, but her description gave her away. When people in the neighborhood read the article, the calls started and the phone hasn't stopped ringing since. They wanted to confirm their guesses. Once they knew Mother thwarted the attempted robbery, flowers and food started arriving, and people have been dropping by all day."

Scott took a dramatic breath and added, "It wouldn't surprise me if that criminal showed up here to cause some trouble."

I couldn't let Scott's drama continue. "He's not going to retaliate. He's already apologized for his foolishness. Besides, everyone from here to California saw his face, too, and knows what he did. I've been getting calls from people in several states. And if I appear on that television talk show, the whole country will know the story!"

"Grandma's going to be on television! Can I be on television with you?" Ryan asked.

"No, I'm not going to be on television. I'm trying to make a point, that's all."

Gretchen interrupted the conversation. "Well, the point to be made is that we could have been visiting you in the hospital if that man would've struck you instead of pushing you to the ground and running out of the store. A wrench is heavy enough to fracture your skull, Mother. You're lucky all he did was knock you down."

I believe Ellen read the desperation on my face, because she came to my rescue in somewhat of a complete turnaround in her thinking. "Well, I'm proud of Mother. I think it's great that she came to that young girl's rescue. And judging from the flowers, cards, and phone calls, a lot of other people think she's a hero, too."

Scott countered. "You're as naïve as she is, Ellen! She could've been killed."

Ellen scoffed. "The man didn't have a gun or knife, and Mother had her heavy cane. Who's to say he wouldn't have knocked her to the ground or hurt her if she had stood by helplessly? Obviously, he lacked common sense if he attempted to rob a store in broad daylight. I say it's better to scare someone off or make an offensive move rather than wait until it's time to defend yourself."

The doorbell rang, interrupting our discussion, and Ryan ran to answer it. "Grandma! Officer Langley is here. He wants to see you."

Gretchen helped me to my walker and escorted me to the door, and the rest of the family followed. Thankfully, Scott stopped the procession and made everyone except Gretchen follow him back to the living room.

"Hi, Gretchen. Hello, Mrs. Higgins. How are you feeling today?"

"Hello, Officer Langley. I'm doing well. The doctor said that I'll be good as new in a few days. I'm a little stiffer than usual, but these old bones are used to creaking."

He laughed. "I won't keep you long. I know you gave a statement at the time of the incident, but I have a couple of additional questions."

Officer Langley reviewed my account of the alleged robbery attempt and the description of the alleged perpetrator. He expressed his gratitude for my involvement and gave me a certificate that read

Super Senior. The certificate included a brief description of my actions. His kindness reassured me that I had done the right thing.

Gretchen and I rejoined the rest of the family. Gretchen waved the certificate in the air, claiming, "It's official! Mother's a 'Super Senior.'"

Ryan interrupted. "Look—Grandma is on television!"

Sure enough, a picture of me flashed on the screen with a news account of the attempted robbery. The newscaster reporting the incident said, "A twenty-nine-year-old tool-wielding suspect was taken into custody for ordering a store clerk to empty her register and give him the cash. An elderly woman who beat the man with her cane foiled the attempted robbery. The would-be robber pushed the woman to the floor, and got away without any money. Fortunately, the woman suffered only minor injuries. The suspect was apprehended a short time later."

Then the cameras flashed to a tall young man with a grim expression.

"That's him!" I shouted. "That's the thief!"

The alleged robber, handcuffed, stood beside a police officer. He spoke quietly to the camera. "I know I apologized before, but I wanted to publicly tell the woman I pushed and the store clerk I scared that I'm very sorry for causing them any harm."

He hung his head while speaking, and his voice sounded sincere. He continued, "I was on drugs at the time and don't remember much about what happened. I know that's no excuse, but I would never hurt someone in my right mind. I need help with my drug problem. I've been addicted for a long time, but I'm willing to accept any help given to me. I want to straighten out my life."

The newscaster wrapped up the story, and we all stared at the television a few minutes longer.

The following Sunday, my pastor congratulated me before the service. Then, after giving his sermon, the pastor announced from the pulpit that he'd love to have a church full of people who would be so ready to help others as I had done.

"And to show Myra our appreciation, the entire congregation is invited to a potluck dinner to honor her. I hope all of you will be able to attend. We're lucky to have her looking out for our interests."

I'm sure my face registered the shock I felt upon hearing the kind words of approval and the dinner invitation. Many of the parishioners approached me after the service and said they would be at the dinner. Even Scott seemed genuinely pleased with the attention I received.

Most of the congregation turned out the night of the dinner. My friends and family made a delicious meal, and the youth group served it. Lena and her manager from the store came, too. The manager presented me with a generous gift certificate to the store and a plaque of appreciation. Lena's parents brought me a special gift to thank me for saving their daughter from a terrible fate. People gave me flowers and gift certificates. I sat at the head table with other members of my family and felt humbled by all the attention.

The pastor asked me to say a few words, and I spoke from my heart. "This town belongs to us and to our children and grandchildren. Protect it against thugs and hoodlums."

I told the audience about all the people before them who worked tirelessly with the local officials to make our home—their home—a place of which we can be proud. There wasn't a sound in the room as I said, "I'm not sure how many times I struck that would-be villain. I only know I hit him as hard as I could, and I'm sure this metal cane got his attention. Hopefully, he had a big headache by the time he got home. He's just lucky I didn't have my walker that day, because he would've really been in trouble, then!"

When the laughter died down, I concluded with words from my heart. "This used to be a thriving community. It brings tears to my eyes to see the condition of things today. We can do better. I challenge every one of you to get out and do something for someone else, to roll up your sleeves and take over for those of us who are too tired and worn out to fight alone. If this old woman can raise a little cane, so can each one of you. It's your town. Take action."

It's been nearly a year since the incident and my life has once again settled into a normal routine. I still get the occasional call, card, or reminder about taking on a thief. I've been referred to as "Gutsy Grandma" more times than I can count. The young man arrested for the attempted robbery has since been charged with the robbery, possession of an instrument of crime, a simple assault charge for hurting me, and reckless endangerment. I attended the hearing at the district court office because I wanted to see justice carried out. A reporter asked me if I felt nervous or afraid attending the hearing, but I didn't.

"If anything, I want to give him a piece of my mind," I told the reporter. "If given the chance, I'd tell him to go get a job like other people do when they need money. I'd tell him to clean up his act and stay off drugs. They have been the downfall of many lives and caused untold grief."

I moved closer to the reporter's microphone. "I'd warn him that he had better look over his shoulder, because concerned citizens like me, who are ready to stop criminals in their tracks, are everywhere. This is my community, and I am sick and tired of thieves and hoodlums recklessly destroying it. And I'm not too old to do something about it!"

THE END

FORCED TO RAISE
MY GRANDBABY

When I had gotten home from work that afternoon, I could tell instantly that something was wrong. Arielle, my seventeen-year-old daughter, was sitting at the kitchen table, looking miserable. I'd set my packages on the kitchen counter.

"What's going on, Arielle? Were you able to find a job?" Even before I'd asked the question, though, I'd known the answer. My daughter had never been reliable. In fact, she'd gone out of her way not to do anything that I'd asked her to do. Since I'd asked her to look for a job a few days before, I knew that she'd probably spent the last few mornings hiding out at her friend's house.

"What's going on, Arielle? Were you able to find a job?" Even before I'd asked the question, though, I'd known the answer. My daughter had never been reliable. In fact, she'd gone out of her way not to do anything that I'd asked her to do. Since I'd asked her to look for a job a few days before, I knew that she'd probably spent the last few mornings hiding out at her friend's house.

As I'd looked into my daughter's sullen eyes, I'd tried to figure out where I'd gone wrong. I'd gotten pregnant with Arielle when I was twenty, and had been forced to raise her alone. Her father, Buck, a guy I'd dated for a few months, had suddenly realized that he'd wanted to serve our country. The last I'd heard of him, he was on a submarine, headed out to sea.

Though I had been young and alone, the prospect of being a single parent hadn't daunted me. Thankfully, my parents had been supportive, and I'd known that I could get a good job. During my pregnancy, I was in my last year of community college. By the time Arielle was born, I'd gotten a secretarial job at a real estate agency. Months after that, I'd passed the test to become a realtor. I'd been selling homes ever since.

By the time Arielle was a year old, I had managed to get us our very own home. But, from the beginning, I could tell that raising my little girl would not be an easy task. She'd thrown tantrums when she didn't get her way. That might have been normal for most children, but Arielle's fits had just seemed a bit extreme. By the time she could form whole sentences, she was calling me names. When she was five, her kindergarten teacher had informed me that I was raising a bully.

The years that followed weren't much better. Arielle, though an intelligent girl, had kept her grades barely high enough to pass each year. Her teachers had constantly complained about her tardiness and bad attitude. When Arielle was fifteen, I'd learned that she'd begun to skip school altogether.

And so, my life was a shambles. Trying to keep my wild child in line had taken up all of my time. I'd had no time to see the few friends that I'd had, and dating was out of the question. I was lonely at home, too, because my daughter rarely spoke to me.

I'd tried everything from tough love, to family therapy, to sending her to live with my parents for a while. Nothing had worked. And so, when Arielle had announced a month earlier that she would not be returning to school, I'd put my foot down. She would not be allowed to lie around the house and watch television. I'd told her to go out and make herself useful.

That evening, I'd pulled out a chair and sat at the table, watching my daughter warily. "What's going on?" I asked.

"I'm pregnant, Mom," she announced finally. "Going on three months."

I'd felt as though the wind had been knocked out of me. I was so surprised that I could not answer her for a minute. This has to be a joke! my mind screamed. You are not hearing this! After a few moments, I was able to compose myself enough to speak to her again. "It's Rick's baby, isn't it?"

She'd grinned, her satisfaction evident. "Yeah—isn't it great? I've known for a few weeks now, but I had to go to the doctor to make sure. Rick's over the moon. He wants me to move in with him."

My first thought was to forbid Arielle to leave. She was seventeen and had no diploma. And what on earth did she know about raising a baby? Yet one thought had brought me back into reality: When has she ever listened to you, Paula? So I'd bitten my lip, asked her if she'd needed any help, and put away the groceries.

Later, I'd called my mother. "I have no idea what to do, Mom. Arielle isn't responsible enough to be a mother."

"You were young when you had Arielle. Paula, don't you forget that. And you did just fine," my mother reminded me, sounding wise.

"Did I, Mom?" I asked. "My daughter treats me more like a landlord than a mother. Except, of course, for the fact that she doesn't pay rent or contribute anything at all. I feel like a stranger in my own home!"

"Give it time, honey. All teenage girls go through this stage. In a few years, the two of you will be best friends."

I'd held my tongue, not wanting to make my mother feel badly. But there was no way that Arielle and I would ever be best friends. I knew it, my mother knew it, and Arielle knew it, too. By that point, I didn't want to be my daughter's friend. I just wanted her to stop treating me as if I was her enemy.

Arielle had been gone for nearly six months when she'd called me one Saturday morning. "Mom, I need you to come and get me. Rick's going crazy. I can't stay here."

Immediately, I'd grabbed my car keys and told her to calm down. "What is it, honey? Are the two of you fighting?"

"I can't explain everything now, Mom. Would you please just drop the twenty questions and get over here?" She'd hesitated, but when I'd heard her voice again, I'd realized that my daughter was scared. "He hit me last night, and when he woke up today, he was still in a bad mood. I'm afraid for the baby."

I'd spent the afternoon collecting Arielle's belongings and trying to keep Rick and her from reconciling. There was no way that I was going to allow my grandchild to be raised in that environment—the apartment was filthy. I'd also suspected that Rick's anger had been triggered by a lot more than a few beers. Was he using drugs?

When the two of us had arrived home, Arielle had seemed less shaken. In fact, I'd soon realized that my efforts were not even especially appreciated.

"I didn't like the way that you were talking to Rick, Mom," she told me haughtily. "I know you don't like him, but he didn't deserve that kind of treatment."

Needless to say, I was stunned. "You're only weeks away from your due date, Arielle. You don't need that kind of stress in your life right now." I'd helped her onto the couch before continuing. "After you have the baby, I'll help you to move back in with him, if that's what you want."

"Really?" My daughter's eyes had brightened.

"Really," I said. "If that's the kind of life you want for you and your child, then by all means, go right on back to it. But the next time you're in trouble, leave me out of it."

I'd realized, even as I'd made that statement that I'd never be able to stick to it. And the worst part was that Arielle had known it, too.

A few weeks later, Arielle had given birth to a beautiful baby girl that she'd named Brittany. The first time that I'd held my granddaughter in my arms, I'd promised her silently that I would make sure that she had a good life—no matter what it cost me.

The first few months after Brittany's birth were good ones. Arielle had seemed genuinely interested in learning to become a good mother. I was also happy to learn that she'd not intended to go back to Rick. She'd decided that she would make it on her own—just as I had. But when it came time for her to look for work, Arielle had dragged her feet.

"I'm doing the best I can!" she yelled one night when I'd asked her if she'd been on any interviews. "Nobody's hiring right now."

"That's not true, Arielle," I told her calmly. "The burger place on Halsey Avenue has had a sign on the window for weeks. And the motel always has openings—"

"I'm not going be a maid, Mom!" she interrupted me. "I'm better than that. And I don't want to be a waitress, either. I want to do office work."

I couldn't help it—I'd laughed. "Office work? You can't even type. I doubt that you know how to use a copy machine."

Arielle had been sitting on the couch when the conversation had started, her foot tapping furiously. Suddenly, she'd stood up and gotten right into my face. "You know what? I'm getting really tired of you telling me what to do. I'm sick of you trying to run my life. I'm a grown woman with a baby. You can't treat me like this!"

I was afraid that if I'd responded, or breathed the wrong way, my daughter would hit me. I'd remained silent as she'd glared at me, her eyes filled with contempt. A moment later, she'd pushed past me, grabbed her leather jacket, and stormed out the back door. I didn't see her again for almost four days.

When Arielle finally had crept back into the house, I was sitting in the dark, waiting for her.

"Don't you ever do that again," I told her after I'd heard her feet moving toward the stairs. "You have Brittany to think about now. Grow up! She cried every day for you, Arielle." Angry tears had run down my face as I'd remembered the long nights that I'd spent cuddling Brittany in my arms, trying to get her to sleep.

Arielle's voice was trembling when she'd answered: "I just needed a few days to myself."

"For what, Arielle?" I asked. "You're a mother now. You don't get any more days to yourself. That part of your life is over—at least until Brittany is an adult." I'd lowered my voice to hide the sarcasm that had bubbled to the surface. "And even your child's adulthood doesn't guarantee days off."

There was a moment of silence so thick that I could have cut it with a knife. I was still sitting in the dark and couldn't see my daughter's face. She could have tiptoed over to the sofa and done anything that she'd wanted to me. I couldn't believe that I'd actually come to fear my own daughter.

One word had broken that horrible silence: "Whatever," she muttered.

I'd heard Arielle run up the stairs and head straight into her room. She hadn't even bothered to ask about the baby.

For weeks after Arielle's first disappearance, I'd watched her like a hawk—sometimes even sneaking into her bedroom at night to make sure that she was still there. But after a while, I was able to lower my guard, especially when it looked like Arielle was trying to be responsible.

"I got a job," she said one day when I came in. "I'm going to be a cashier at a music store."

I'd beamed. "That's great, Arielle. When do you start?"

"Monday. I'm kind of excited, I guess. I've never had a real job before." She'd stood up and hugged me.

And yet, our happy moment hadn't lasted. "When you get your first check, we'll decide how to budget it for you," I told her. "Of course, you can finally help out with the food, and the phone, and—"

"You act like I'm going to be making lots of money or something, Mom," she interrupted me. "The job barely pays above minimum wage." Disgusted, Arielle had pointed a finger at me. "I need new clothes and CDs and a DVD player."

I must have blanked out on the rest because I couldn't honestly remember any more of what my daughter had said in that moment. Where had I gone wrong? I'd tried so hard to stress upon Arielle the importance of responsibility and independence, and yet, it had seemed as though she hadn't been listening. She'd gotten the job for one reason and for one reason only—to buy things for herself. No mention of baby Brittany. No mention of contributing to the household expenses in any way.

After she'd rambled on for what had seemed like a half hour, I'd interrupted her. "You're something else, Arielle. I mean, I know you couldn't care less about me, but the fact that your child means so little to you is something else entirely." Swept up in my emotions, I'd grabbed my child's arms, thinking that, maybe, I could shake some sense into her. "What's happened to you? Why are you like this? How can I help you?"

Her eyes had flashed and there was no mistaking the hate in them. Not only could I see her hatred for me, but I could feel it, too. I'd let her go at that moment—physically and emotionally. My child was damaged. None of my love or hope mattered to that selfish young woman. Arielle did not want or need me. Except, of course, when she'd wanted a baby-sitter, or someone to cook her dinner.

Before she could respond to my pleas, I'd turned away. There was just no way that I could bring myself to look into her face again. She had become like a stranger to me—a stranger that I did not like very much.

"Fine, Arielle. You don't want to do anything around here? You don't want to contribute? Then you'll have to leave," I told her.

"No problem." Arielle had glowered at me. "Brittany and I will be out of here before you know it."

I'd turned back to face her, wanting her to see the look on my face. "If you leave, you leave alone. I will not let you take that child out of this house."

"She's mine. You can't stop me!" Arielle's face was bright red with anger. "I have rights."

"You have the right to be a good mother. You have the right to keep a job, and to provide for yourself and your baby. If you won't do those things, Arielle, then you might as well leave Brittany with me."

Arielle's eyes had narrowed and she'd appeared to think about what I'd said. Had I finally gotten through to her? "I'm sorry if I seem selfish, Mom—" she began.

"You are selfish, Arielle," I insisted.

"Okay." She'd reached forward and grabbed my hands. "I am selfish. I just had no idea how much my life would change once I had Brittany. But I swear that I'll try to be a better mother." Releasing my hands, my daughter had stepped forward and placed her hands upon my shoulders. "And a better daughter."

I'd wanted so badly to believe her.

And, for a while, Arielle had made it easy for me to believe in her. She'd gone to work every day—sometimes even working extra shifts. She'd helped with the bills and taken a greater interest in Brittany's welfare. Even on the odd nights when Arielle had gone out for a little fun, I'd begun to trust her to be back at a decent hour. I was proud of her progress, though I could never bring myself to tell her. I was afraid that my praise would send her running in the other direction.

One thing I did worry about, though, was the fact that she was dating again. I hadn't met Jesse, but if her past history was any indicator, I knew that I probably wouldn't like him.

My daughter liked him, though—too much. Arielle had begun to sit by the phone every night, waiting for his call. Even her diet had changed. No more fast-food lunches—all she'd ever touched in those days were salads and steaming cups of black coffee.

Yes, life had been very good for a while. But about a week before Brittany's first birthday, my mother had passed away. She'd managed to hold on for a whole three years after my father's death, but, finally, she'd succumbed to a stroke in her sleep.

I was beside myself with grief—and I was overwhelmed with making the final arrangements. I couldn't count on my older brother, John, even to come home—much less to help me out. He was ten years older than I was, and he had left home—and the country—when I was seven. I'd only seen him five times since then.

After my mother's death, I'd turned to Arielle for assistance. "Honey, can you call up the funeral home and check on the casket?" I asked. "The owner swore that it would arrive at the funeral home this afternoon, but he didn't sound too sure to me."

But Arielle had other plans—more important things on her mind. "Don't worry about it, Mom. I'm sure that the guy's taking care of it."

My nerves were so frayed by that time, I supposed my response was short. "I didn't ask you that, Arielle. I asked you to call and make sure."

I'd watched my daughter move toward the stairs. "I can't, Mom. I have to feed Brittany. And, after that, I'm going out with Jesse." She'd taken a few steps before turning toward me again. "And don't wait up!"

I hadn't had the energy to chase her down for one of our old fights, so I'd made the call myself. And yet, Arielle's attitude had bothered me. By the day of the funeral, my feelings had intensified. Right before we'd left for the service, Arielle had told me that she had plans to go out with Jesse. She'd announced that she would leave right after we'd been to the cemetery.

"I don't think so, Arielle!" I snapped. "You know that we have guests coming over after the funeral. I need you to help serve. Plus, I just can't handle baby-sitting today."

She'd tossed back her hair and pulled down her too-short black dress. I'd had to bite my tongue when I'd seen what she was wearing. "I won't be gone long, Mom. I promise."

"But I need you here today, Arielle. Why can't you be there for me? I need you here!" I insisted.

"What you need, Mom, is to chill out. I know that you're upset that Grandma died, but it was for the best. She was old—and she was so lonely since Grandpa died. And now you won't have to worry about her so much."

Before I'd realized what I'd done, my hand had lashed out and connected with her cheek. "Don't you ever speak about your grandmother that way! She did so much for us—for you. How can you say those things?"

Arielle had rubbed her cheek and backed away, a wild look in her eyes. "That's just the excuse I needed, Mom. You can go to the funeral by yourself. I won't be there!" She'd stormed out the front door, slamming it hard behind her.

I couldn't go after her. I was too afraid of what I might say—too afraid of what I might do. My daughter hadn't changed one bit—she was the same ungrateful brat that she had always been. She was pleasant only when things were going her way.

The rest of the day had ended the way that it had begun—miserably. Brittany had cried all day, desperately looking for her mommy. I'd lost count of how many times I had to explain Arielle's absence. I'd lied, of course, saying that she just couldn't take the time off from work. I was too humiliated to let anyone know that she hadn't cared enough to pay her final respects to her own grandmother.

But, in time, I would run out of excuses for my daughter. Soon, everyone in town would know the truth about Arielle.

When Arielle came home—a full day after I'd buried my mother—she'd headed to her bedroom immediately and begun to pack her bags. "I can't live here anymore," she announced as I'd looked in from the doorway. "I'm leaving now. And if you try to stop me from taking the baby, I'll call the police."

I'd felt so many emotions rush through me in that moment—fear, relief, anger, trepidation. I'd felt like a bad mother. Part of me was happy that Arielle was leaving. But I was fearful for Brittany, too. My grandchild was an innocent victim, but there was nothing that I could do for her legally. Arielle was still Brittany's mother.

"Take care of Brittany, Arielle. And yourself," I said simply. I'd turned to go back to my room. "Don't hesitate to call if you need me, honey."

From behind me, I'd heard Arielle laugh harshly. "I won't need you. My days of needing you are over."

And just like that, my daughter had walked out of my life, taking my granddaughter with her.

The days that had followed were nearly impossible to endure. Every time the phone rang or the doorbell chimed, I'd thought that it was Arielle. But she'd never called or stopped by. It was almost as if she'd dropped off the face of the earth. I wasn't even sure if she'd still lived in our small town, or in the surrounding area.

When I'd closed my eyes at night, I'd often have nightmares about my granddaughter waking up to an empty house, or of Arielle trying to make her way back home. I'd started knitting because sleeping was something that I'd become afraid to do. I'd also prayed a lot. God was the only sane thing in my life.

Yet, slowly, as the months had passed, I'd begun to take back my life. I'd looked up old friends and spent time with them. I'd learned to bowl, and I was involved with the women's circle at church. By the time that Arielle had been gone nearly a year, I'd met a nice man. Vince was a divorced father of three who'd owned his own auto body business. He was kind and sympathetic and would listen for hours as I'd talked about my problems with Arielle. Not only was he a great boyfriend, but he'd grown to become my best friend.

One afternoon as Vince and I were preparing to go out for an early dinner, the telephone had rung. I'd thought that perhaps it was Connie, my bowling buddy, calling to make sure that we were still on for our next game. But when I'd picked up the phone, I'd heard my daughter's voice.

"Mom? It's Arielle," she began.

71

My legs were so weak that I'd had to sit down on the sofa before I could bring myself to answer. "How are you, honey?" But of course, I'd known what she would say. Arielle would only have called me if something were terribly wrong.

"I'm not doing so well, Mom. I'm in the hospital over in Greendale. I need you to come up here and get Brittany."

My hand had tightened around the telephone at the sound of my baby's voice. Her breathing had sounded so labored—her voice so far away. What on earth had happened to her? "I'll be there as soon as I can, baby—okay? Don't you worry. I'm on my way."

Vince had been in the bathroom when Arielle had called. After quickly explaining the situation, we'd jumped into his car and driven to Greendale, a little town over ninety miles away. During the year that she'd been gone, I'd had no idea that my daughter was still living so close by.

When we'd arrived at the hospital, I was shocked by what I'd found. Arielle had been beaten savagely. Her hair had been pulled out in chunks, and a few of her teeth were missing. She had also lost a lot of weight. If her name had not been on her hospital wristband, I would never have believed that the wreck of a woman before me was my daughter.

"Honey?" I couldn't hide the tears that were pouring down my face. I was so glad that I'd asked Vince to wait outside. "Baby, what happened to you? Who did this to you? Was it Jesse?"

Arielle looked up at me as best as she could, considering that her eyes were tight slits. "No, it was Jay. Jay got angry and said that I stole his drugs. But I didn't—"

I'd listened in horror as Arielle had rambled on about Jay and a drug deal gone wrong. It was obvious that Arielle had gotten herself involved with some bad people. I couldn't say that I was surprised. But where was Brittany?

"Honey—" I'd sat down on the edge of her bed and put my fingers against her lips to get her attention. "Where is Brittany? Who's taking care of the baby?"

Arielle had started coughing, and she hadn't been able to stop for some time. It seemed to have taken all of her strength for her to speak to me. "I left her with my friend, Leanne. Leanne's got a two-year-old boy. Brian and Brittany play together."

I'd wanted to be relieved, yet I knew that if Leanne ran with the same crowd that my daughter did, Brittany could be in danger. "Give me her address, Arielle," I ordered.

When we'd arrived, I'd seen that the tiny, two-room apartment was a shambles. Pizza boxes, beer cans, and paper plates littered the floor, and the television was blaring. Leanne, the young woman

72

who'd opened the door, had smiled and asked us to sit down. "Well, it isn't a palace, but it's all I can afford. Do you want a drink?"

Vince shook his head. "No, thank-you," he told her. "We just came to pick up Brittany. She's Paula's granddaughter."

Leanne had looked at me for a minute. "Wow, Arielle looks just like you." She'd gestured toward a window. "The kids are out back playing."

"Will you show us?" I asked.

Leanne had led us out to the back and I was both stunned and horrified by what I'd seen. Brittany was a lot bigger than the last time I'd seen her, but not big enough. She was taller, but too thin. Her hair was filthy and her clothes looked like they hadn't been washed in weeks. I'd bitten my lip to hold back tears of anger. My granddaughter had looked like an abandoned child.

Vince and Leanne had stayed back as I'd approached the children. My first thought was that Brittany probably wouldn't remember me. It had been a year, and children could lose memories so quickly. Would she hesitate to come with me?

"Brittany," I said, bending down. "It's your grandma, honey. Your mommy sent me here to pick you up."

The little girl had stood up and dusted off her hands. Then she'd looked me over, up and down. Finally, she'd extended her little hand. "I remember you," she said. Her words were so clear—so mature. I'd almost broken down right then. Though she'd looked as though she'd been through hard times, Brittany hadn't been damaged. I could still save her.

"I remember you, too, Brittany. I've missed you very much."

"Mommy told me that we couldn't see you. That made me sad," she told me.

I'd picked her up and pulled her into my arms. "You don't have to feel sad anymore, honey. I'm taking you home."

And that's exactly what I did.

Though I'd told Arielle about my plans while she was still in the hospital, she was angry when she was finally released a week later. "Thanks for watching Brittany and everything, Mom, but I'll be there in a couple of days to pick her up," she informed me.

I hadn't hesitated to respond. "Don't bother about that right now, honey. What I want you to concentrate on is getting treatment so that you can get your life together."

"My life is just fine, Mom." Arielle's voice was high-pitched. "On second thought, I'll come down and pick up Brittany today."

"I won't let you take her, Arielle. You're a drug addict—you can barely take care of yourself. I shouldn't have let you take her in the first place." My hands were trembling. "And I won't let you take her now—or ever again."

Arielle didn't say anything for a while. I'd thought that, perhaps, she would see the sense in what I was saying. But as had been the case in the past concerning my daughter, I was wrong. "Listen, Mom, if you try to keep my daughter away from me, I'll make you sorry! Do not mess with me—do you hear me? When I come over there, I expect her to be ready to go."

I wouldn't fight with her, but I wouldn't change my mind, either. "No, Arielle. I'll fight to keep her."

"But you can't win! I'm her mother!" she yelled.

"You're an unfit mother, Arielle! What kind of mother leaves her baby in a drug addict's apartment? What kind of mother gets beaten up and winds up in the hospital after a drug deal? And I know the police are looking at you—do you think that they'll hesitate to help me?"

I'd listened as Arielle hurled curses and other filth at me. "I know people who would kill you as soon as look at you, Mom," she threatened. "Do you really want me to start making calls? Calling in favors? I can make your life miserable."

"Not as miserable as your life, Arielle. And I'll chance whatever it is you think that you can throw at me. I couldn't save you, but I'm going to do my best to save your daughter." Even though I'd realized that it was impossible, I'd reached out to my child one last time. "Won't you help me to help your child? You might hate me, but I know that you love Brittany. Why won't you allow me to help her?"

"Because she doesn't need it, you witch! She's mine—the only thing that I've got. And I'm not letting you take her away. You already ruined my life. I'm not going to let you do the same thing to Brittany."

Knowing that I couldn't reason with her, I'd hung up. Later that night, I'd gone into my granddaughter's room and tucked her in. I'd promised her that I would protect her from anything and everything in the world that could hurt her—especially her mother.

For days after that, Arielle had called the house to scream obscenities. Sometimes, she'd just hang up. Other times, a male voice would call.

"Hey, Paula. I was thinking of coming down there to pay you a visit. And to pick up little Brittany," the voice would threaten.

I'd hang up, but I was a nervous wreck. I couldn't go anywhere or do anything because I was afraid of leaving Brittany alone for a second. Vince would stop by after work with takeout and toys for Brittany. During that terrible time, I'd realized what a gem he was.

After about three weeks, the phone calls had stopped. I hoped that Arielle had finally given up. More importantly, I'd hoped that she'd realized that allowing her child to live with me was the best thing—at least for a while. But when my doorbell rang one afternoon,

74

I'd realized that Arielle would not take the situation lying down.

"Where is she?" Arielle screamed, looking ready to run over me if she'd had to. "Get her ready to leave—now! She's going home with her mother."

Arielle had looked as though she was ready for a fight, so when I'd asked her to come in and take a seat, she'd looked surprised.

"We have to talk, Arielle. And we're going to do it today."

My daughter's eyes had darted around. "Is that guy here?"

"Vince is at work. It's just you and me, Arielle. Let's go into the kitchen." I'd put on some tea. "You know, just because you've destroyed your life doesn't give you the right to destroy Brittany's. Why can't you see that, Arielle?"

"She's mine. I have a right to her," she insisted.

"But why, Arielle? What do you want with her? It seems to me that she hinders your lifestyle quite a bit. Wouldn't it be easier to run the streets without a little girl to support and worry about?"

She'd crossed her arms across her chest. "You let me worry about that stuff, Mom. You're a free woman now. You don't need some kid weighing you down." Arielle had accepted the tea that I'd placed in front of her. "Besides, look at how great I turned out."

I'd laughed bitterly. "You think that it's my fault that you've turned out this way? I tried everything to keep you on the right road. You were determined to do things your own way. I won't accept the blame for that, Arielle." I'd stood up and pulled a document out of the kitchen drawer. "I want you to sign this."

"What is it?" Arielle's eyes had scanned the document and grown wider at every line. "No way! No way am I giving up my rights to Brittany!"

"You don't and I'll drag you through the courts for as long as I have to, even if it's up until that child's eighteenth birthday. I'll use your past against you, Arielle. I understand that you've got yourself quite a nice rap sheet. How do you think a judge will respond to that?"

Angry tears had sprung to Arielle's eyes. "You'd do that? You'd do that to your own daughter?"

"In a heartbeat, Arielle," I assured her. "I'll do whatever I can to make sure that Brittany has a chance at a decent life. There's no way that she's going to get that with you."

My daughter had jumped up so quickly that I'd almost fallen in my hurry to get out of her way. "I should kill you, Mom. I should just take one of those knives and let you have it."

I hadn't backed down. "If you do that, Brittany will wind up in the system. And I'd still rather that she grow up in foster homes than take a chance on living with you."

Arielle's lips had trembled, but she'd appeared to make up her mind about something. She'd moved back to the table and asked for a pen. "I'll sign this, but I want you to promise me that when I get better, you'll let me have her back."

I shook my head. "I'll let you see her—maybe. But I won't promise that she'll ever be able to live with you again, Arielle. Just sign the papers. It's the best thing for everyone."

Hands shaking, Arielle had signed the papers. I hadn't realized that I'd been holding my breath until she was finished. She'd looked at me, her eyes filled with tears. "I'm sorry, Mom. I really am." Then she'd opened the back door and left.

The years that followed have been tough and sweet all at the same time. Brittany is five now and in kindergarten. Her teachers report that she's an excellent student, who gets along well with her classmates. Vince, who stuck by me throughout that stressful time, will be soon become my husband. Brittany loves him, and thinks of him as her grandfather.

I've not heard from nor talked to Arielle since that day in the kitchen. I think about my daughter every day and wonder about her. Is she healthy . . . safe? Is she alive? All I know for sure is that I've finally gotten over my guilt about not being able to save her. I still love my child. And, if she needed it, I'd help her in a minute. But I no longer torture myself about my failings as a mother. With Brittany, I have a chance to mold her into a whole person—a young woman with respect, will, and a drive to do something with her life. She's what I concentrate on now.

The funny thing is that I'd always thought that I was the one who was saving Brittany. But I know now that I've been so wrong. Her spirit and her love is what has saved me.

THE END

A GRANDDAUGHTER IS
A KISS FROM HEAVEN
We are raising her—and loving it

I was feeling very satisfied with my life. The house was clean, supper was in the oven, and I had time to put my feet up with a good book. A new historical romance had been beckoning to me all afternoon.

A few minutes later I heard the back door open and my youngest son hollered, "Mom? Are you here?" Married and with three children of his own, I was grateful he'd settled in the small city where we lived. It gave us time to spend with these grandchildren—time we didn't have with the grandchildren who lived farther away.

I laid my book on the table in the kitchen where Bobby stood holding a big, green garbage bag.

"Hi, guys," I said as my eleven-year-old granddaughter appeared at his heels. "What a nice surprise."

A good look at Chelsea stopped me from saying more. She was staring at the floor, her hair falling forward to screen her face.

"Can Chelsea stay with you for a while?" my son asked, his gaze directed somewhere past my shoulder.

"Of course she can," I replied instantly. "Is something wrong?"

Bobby dropped the bag on the kitchen floor and gestured toward his daughter. "I don't know all the details," he said, still avoiding my eyes, "but some people from Social Services showed up this afternoon to ask Brittany questions about Chelsea. Seems like she told the school counselor she was being mistreated at home, so now we're being investigated and Brittany's really upset."

Brittany was upset? Had he looked at his daughter's face?

"I have to get back home," he said as he headed for the back door. "I'll let you know when . . . when I know more about what's going on."

With that, he was gone.

"Chelsea?" I said softly. She threw her arms around my waist and sobbed as if her heart were breaking. I felt like joining her.

Finally I picked up the garbage bag and said, "Let's put your things in the guest room. Grandpa will be so happy to see you when he gets home." I led the way down the hall. Chelsea could have the guest room and the empty bedroom I'd set up with all my sewing things would have to do for any unexpected company we might have.

77

I busied myself emptying a couple of drawers and dumped the contents of the garbage bag on the floor.

Bobby and Brittany, his second wife, had two little boys ages one and five in addition to Chelsea. It wouldn't be fair to say that I didn't like Brittany—I'd admired the way she worked full time and still managed to keep a household going. We were never close but her mother lived nearby and Britt was naturally closer to her own mother.

Seeing Chelsea's clothing spread out in front me, I felt a prickle of anger growing in my stomach. Brittany always said that she could find lots of clothes in Chelsea's size at garage sales but nothing that fit the two little boys. I admired her thriftiness because I knew money was very tight. What I never wanted to look too closely at was the fact that this had continued for several years—and it was always Chelsea's size that was the only one available at garage sales and thrift shops.

Chelsea put her clothes in the drawers I'd emptied while I put fresh sheets on the daybed. Out of the corner of my eye I could see that her things took up pitifully little room in the space I'd cleared—no personal items, no toys—just faded, well-worn clothes, and not many of them.

We'd no more than finished when I heard Al's truck in the driveway. Chelsea heard it, too, and her face lit up like a hundred-watt bulb. She raced to the back door and I heard her squeal as Al gave her a bear hug that lifted her off the floor. It was their ritual, begun when she was a tiny child.

When I entered the kitchen, my husband looked at me over Chelsea's head and raised his brows in question. I shook my head, our signal for "later," and opened the cupboard to get glasses and plates.

"While I finish fixing dinner, Chelsea, would you like to take a bubble bath?" Before she could ask, I said, "Since tonight is your first night with us, I think you can wear your nightclothes to the table."

"Oh, yes," Chelsea said, twirling around. "Do you still have some of that Sweet Pea I used the last time I was here?"

"I sure do, honey, and some others, too. Come on. I'll show you." Bottles of inexpensive bubble bath had become something special to all our grandchildren when they spent the night.

Chelsea gathered her robe and pajamas while I started the water running. Once I was sure she was occupied for a few minutes, I went back to the kitchen.

Al was at the sink, filling the coffeemaker. "Well? What's that all about?"

His face darkened as I repeated what little I knew. I summed it all up with, "So until they sort it all out, Chelsea is staying with us."

"What is wrong with those two?" he exploded.

"Hush. Do you want Chelsea to hear you?"

"I'm sure she's heard plenty by now, if things have reached a point where they want her out of the house." Al sat down on a chair at the kitchen table. "I'll have a talk with that son of ours." His anger radiated in almost-visible waves.

I sat down across from him. "I hope you'll wait until you cool down. I really think we need to be calm when we do talk to him, to let him know that we love them and we just want to help."

He picked up on only one phrase. "Why wait?" He was impatient to do something and I understood the impulse.

I summoned all my half-remembered parenting skills. "Something is very wrong, honey. To discard Chelsea like an unwanted kitten? It isn't like Bobby. You know how hard he fought Chelsea's mother for custody. I have to believe he really wants what's best for his daughter."

I pulled my thoughts back from those painful days and tried to choose the right words. "Maybe this is best for now. Chelsea's happy here and it isn't a problem for us to have her. Maybe we should let things ride and see what develops."

"You may be right," he said with a rueful grin. "Sometimes you are, you know."

The next few days fell into a routine. Al dropped Chelsea off at school each morning and Bobby picked her up and delivered her back to our house in the afternoon. I picked up some things for Chelsea when I was shopping—a few clothes, colored pencils, puzzles, and more bubble bath. The fact that no one had bothered to pack any of Chelsea's toys or personal belongings made me heartsick. Was the situation in our son's house so bad that he had to grab whatever was at hand and whisk Chelsea away? My hands began to shake as I put away the few things I bought.

It was all well and good for me to tell Al to cool down but waiting was having the opposite effect on me. I began to remember things, too: How I felt something uncomfortable nibble at me when Brittany fixed up the baby's room with special matching curtains and bedding while Chelsea had only a window shade and old, chenille bedspread in her room. And again when the boys took karate lessons but Chelsea couldn't take ballet dancing because it would require a second trip. In our town, a second trip amounts to a three- or four-minute drive.

When Chelsea arrived home the next day, she came into the kitchen where I was peeling potatoes and hung her book bag from a hook by the back door.

"Hi, sweetie," I said, turning from the sink. "How did school go today?"

"Okay," she said with typical eleven-year-old enthusiasm. "Grandma?"

Something in her voice made an alarm go off in my head. "What is it, honey?"

"I forgot to ask you about my chores."

My face must've reflected my confusion because she elaborated, "You know, chores. Like I did at home." A frown like a small cloud crossed her face.

"What did you do at home?" I asked.

"Well," she said, ticking off the jobs on her fingers, "every day after school I had to shake out the throw rugs, use a dry mop on the kitchen and dining room floors and then a wet mop, pick up the living room, and vacuum the carpet." She stopped for a second, staring at her still-folded thumb. "Oh—and empty and load the dishwasher."

"Every day?" I asked, thinking my own housekeeping wasn't nearly as meticulous.

"Those were my after-school chores," she said matter-of-factly. "Before school I had to watch the baby while Mom took her bath, make my bed, make Dakota's breakfast, and feed the dog." She paused. "And on the weekends I had to strip all the beds, make them up with fresh sheets, catch up on the laundry, and watch the boys so Mom could do stuff. So what do you want me to do, Grandma?"

I hadn't thought about it but our kids all had chores to do and of course Chelsea needed them, too. But that list of chores? Surely even the most truthful child sometimes exaggerates. "Let me think about it for a while, honey. I'll give you an answer tonight, okay?"

By nightfall I had a list for Chelsea: Do your homework, clean your room once a week, and unload the dishwasher daily.

At the beginning of the second week, I was surprised when Bobby followed Chelsea into the kitchen. She stared straight ahead and went on into her room without a word. My inner alarm system sent shrill warnings along my spine.

"Hi, Mom," Bobby said as he kissed my cheek and sank onto a kitchen chair with a weary sigh. He put his elbows on the table and rubbed his eyes. The night shift was wearing on any who tried to keep a schedule that allowed them to see their families—and a lot of people in our town showed the effects.

"Coffee, honey?"

"Sure. That sounds good."

I poured a mug half-full and put the sugar bowl and milk on the table next to him. We always teased Bobby that his coffee was half milk and sweet enough to produce cavities—he didn't drink it black like the rest of the family.

I poured a cup for myself and sat down across from him. No matter how angry I might get at my children's actions, I couldn't hold on to that feeling. When I saw them, all I could remember was how much I loved them and how much I wanted them to be happy. Bobby's face was scored with lines I hadn't seen a few weeks ago. Questions tumbled through my mind, mixing with flashes of memories. He stirred in several spoonfuls of sugar and filled the mug to the brim with milk. Then he held it between his hands, staring into it as if was about to produce answers he needed.

"Grandma?" Chelsea spoke from behind my chair.

"Yes, honey?"

"Can I go next door and see if Emma can play?"

"I can't think of any reason why you shouldn't," I said with relief. I didn't want to discuss anything with my son while his daughter was in earshot.

"Thanks, Grandma. I love you." Chelsea hugged me around my neck with one arm and with a wary glance at her dad, went out the back door.

The room grew silent as I waited for Bobby to say what he'd obviously come to say. Finally he glanced up but didn't meet my eyes before he looked down at his cup again. "We're going to see a family counselor tomorrow. Brittany will pick Chelsea up about six-thirty and we'll be back before her bedtime."

I nodded my head. A family counselor wouldn't be a bad idea. Maybe an objective outsider could make sense of all this since I certainly couldn't.

"Mom?" Bobby's voice caught and he cleared his throat. "I feel like I'm caught in the middle and I don't know what to do." He put his mug down and flattened his hands on the tabletop. "I love Chelsea, you know that. And I love Brittany and the boys. I don't want to lose any of them."

I pushed my coffee away. "I know, Bobby. And I know this is hard for you, as hard maybe as it is for Chelsea." He looked up at me with tear-glazed eyes. All this pain and no easy way out. "Someday you'll look back and this will be in the past. All we can do is try to make the best choices we can right now to do as little damage to everyone as possible." I covered his hand with mine. "Your dad and I love you, Bobby, and we'll do whatever we can to help."

"Thanks, Mom," he said, rubbing his hands over his face. "I'll let you know how it goes with the counselor. I sure hope she can produce a miracle or two."

He gave me a hug and after he went out the door I could hear his voice and Chelsea's in the yard. "Bye, Dad!" she called out as his car pulled away from the curb. "See you tomorrow."

I put our cups in the sink and rinsed them out. He said he didn't want to lose any of them. That could only mean that Brittany was threatening to take the boys and leave him. It was going to take a miracle.

In bed that night, I explained to Al about the family counseling session.

Al sighed. "I'm glad they're doing something before it's too late. I think I'll stay in the garage when Brittany comes for Chelsea. Right now I don't trust myself to be able to stay calm if I have to see her and I don't want to make things any worse."

"You know, we blame Brittany but Bobby is just as guilty for letting this happen."

"I know," he said, punching his pillow into shape. "I thought I knew Bobby, but. . . . It's hard to believe my own son could treat his daughter like this."

The next day I tried to distract myself by finishing an order for a dress. It was for a little flower girl in a wedding and I had to concentrate to keep the organza under control. The mesmerizing effect of watching the fabric disappear beneath the pressure-foot of the machine gave my mind time to wander.

Instead of keeping me from thinking about the coming meeting with Brittany, the repetitious action let my mind project a variety of scenarios for the coming afternoon—not all of them pleasant. I finally convinced myself that Brittany would probably want to mend this rift as soon as possible, just as we did. Finally I went to Chelsea's room and made a list of things we might shop for to make it more like a little girl's room.

When she came home from school, Chelsea was unnaturally quiet. She did her homework without being reminded and sat on the back steps visiting with the little girl from next door. She changed her clothes after an early supper and spent some time agonizing over what to wear. She finally settled on a pair of jeans with pink trim, and a pink sweater I purchased the weekend before.

At twenty minutes after six, Brittany's little blue Honda pulled up at the curb. She left the two boys in the car. I opened the door and went out on the porch to meet her. Chelsea came out of the garage and went down the walk. Brittany said something I couldn't hear and pointed at the car. Then she came up the steps where I was standing.

"Is Al here?" she demanded.

"He's in the garage."

She pushed past me. "I want to talk to him."

"Now wouldn't be a good time, Brittany," I said. Why did she want to see Al? "He's really not feeling very—"

"I don't care whether it's a good time or not. I'm going to talk to him." She marched through the door.

It was her decision but I didn't have to stay and witness the fallout. "I'll sit in the car with the kids," I said to her retreating back. I opened the door of Brittany's car and slid into the backseat with the two boys.

82

"Grandma, Grandma," little Jacob cried, waving his fists from his car seat.

"Hi, Grandma," Dakota said, flashing a pleased grin. "Jacob and me are going to my other grandma's to play. Mommy and Daddy are going to the doctor and Chelsea has to go with them." He lowered his voice to a whisper. "Is Chelsea sick, Grandma?"

"No, sweetie," I replied, "she isn't sick. I think they're just going to talk for a while." He seemed satisfied with my explanation but my stomach was churning.

In the front seat, Chelsea was silent, her listening antennas all but visible. I scrambled for a subject to occupy the boys. I didn't know much about Pokémon, Blue's Clues, or Dora the Explorer anymore, but occasionally Al tuned in to SpongeBob cartoons. "Have you seen SpongeBob, lately? Or has he been busy teaching his other friends how to behave?"

"Oh, Grandma. You're being silly." Dakota grinned in response to my teasing.

The breezeway door flew open. Brittany swooped down the driveway toward us and Al appeared in the open doorway behind her.

Brittany swung around on the walk to face him and shrieked, "You think you know everything, you jerk! And your son is just like you!"

I patted Dakota's hand and stepped out of the car, shutting the door firmly behind me. It was probably futile to hope that I could prevent the children from hearing anything more.

Brittany brushed by me as she rounded the back of the car. "I'll be so glad when I never have to see you people again," she muttered.

She slammed the car into gear and pulled away. Chelsea didn't look up as I waved.

My feet felt like they were encased in concrete. Al opened the storm door for me when I reached the porch. "What was that all about?" I asked as we entered the living room.

He slumped down in his recliner. "I'll give you the condensed, PG-rated version." He scrubbed both hands over his face as if trying to rub away the memory. "Brittany wanted me to know that everything is our fault. She says we spoiled Bobby, she thinks we favor Chelsea over the boys. Linda—" he looked up at me. "The hatred in that girl. . . . She blames Chelsea for everything that has ever gone wrong in that house and what she doesn't blame Chelsea for is our fault. Britt thinks Chelsea deliberately tried to cause trouble for her—that Chelsea hates her—and she doesn't ever want her in their house again. She even called Chelsea a bad seed. Did you ever imagine Britt being childish?"

I shook my head. "No, I don't suppose I did, but then I never imagined anything like this happening—not in our family."

Later, after I cleaned up the kitchen, I stepped out onto the patio. I did some of my best thinking while working in the yard but the ground was too wet to do anything now.

"Linda. Linda! Over here." My neighbor beckoned from the fence that divided our yards. Though she was young enough to be my daughter, we'd been friends for years—a shared interest in needlework had been the catalyst. Her daughter, Emma, was Chelsea's frequent playmate.

"You look tired," she said as I approached the fence. There weren't any secrets between us and she knew how stressful the last weeks had been. "Is it Chelsea?"

I explained about the counseling session and a little of Brittany's explosion.

"I hope the sessions help," she said, "but I doubt it will do much good."

I was surprised. "Why is that?"

"Emma tells me one of her friends at school repeated something her mother said, and her mother is a friend of Brittany's." At my questioning look, she continued, "The little girl said she heard her mother telling her dad that Brittany has already turned Chelsea's old room into a bedroom for the baby, instead of having the two boys share a room. It sounds like Brittany doesn't plan to ever have Chelsea live with them again."

My stomach sank like a lead weight and I shook my head. "I honestly don't know what Brittany thinks, but I'm afraid it's Chelsea who's going to get hurt." She nodded in sympathy and changed the subject.

A few minutes later I went back to the house and found Al staring at the television. He patted the cushion next to him and I sat down. His arm settled around my shoulders and he pulled me close before pressing his lips to the top of my head.

"Don't worry, hon," he murmured. "It will all turn out the way it's supposed to."

My husband's reminder settled the discomfort stirring in my stomach and I relaxed. He was right. We had to trust that things would work out. That, and do our best.

When Chelsea returned, I heard the car pull away as she opened the back door. She hung up her jacket and came into the living room. "I asked Britt for my books and my music box, but she said the boys were using them so I couldn't have them," she blurted out.

Al and I stared at each other in silence. "How did things go with the counselor?" I asked as she sank onto the seat next to me.

"Okay, I guess. The lady talked to each of us separately and then together but that didn't work so good because no one wanted to say anything when we were all in the same room."

Al shifted on the other side of me. "Come give me a hug," he said to Chelsea. She slid in between us and pressed her head against his chest. "Did you like the counselor?" he asked with a hopeful tone in his voice.

"She was all right," Chelsea said. "I told her I missed my brothers. But then she asked me where I want to live."

"What did you tell her?" Al asked as I held my breath.

"I told her I like it better here because there is a lot of love in this house."

Tears stung my eyes. "Let's have some milk and cookies before you go to bed." A grandma's solution to everything.

Later, when we were in bed, I turned to Al and said, "What if the way this is supposed to turn out is that we're meant to raise Chelsea?"

Al snorted as if he couldn't believe I'd even ask. "Then we raise Chelsea," he said, pulling me to him. I blessed the power that sent me this man.

Two days later I took my courage in hand and called the counselor whose name Chelsea had given me.

"Because of privacy issues, I can't tell you anything," she said when she came on the line.

"I understand that. But I want to tell you something."

"Yes?" Her voice was tentative.

"My husband and I only want to help. We hate seeing our family in pain. We just want you to know that we're willing to do whatever we can. All you have to do is ask."

The line was silent for a moment. Then she said, "This is a typical Cinderella story and I'm glad you're there for your granddaughter. Thank you for calling." The line went dead.

Cinderella. It was nice to know I wasn't crazy for all the things I'd been thinking but it didn't make the situation look any brighter. Cinderella's stepmother was definitely willing to sacrifice a stepdaughter in order to put her own children first.

The next days passed quickly and my pile of unread books didn't diminish. Chelsea wanted to learn to knit so I found some heavy yarn and large needles for her to practice with. We baked cookies and she had her friends in to play. We started sorting old photographs I'd been meaning to put in albums and I found myself telling her family stories as we sorted the photos.

In the middle of the week, Chelsea called Brittany to tell her that Bobby wouldn't have to pick her up after school on Friday because Chelsea was going home with a friend to spend the night. When she hung up the phone, her eyes were suspiciously shiny.

"What is it, sweetie?"

"Brittany says it's nice enough weather now that I should just walk home from school from now on." She looked at the floor and then up at me. "I don't think she wants me to see my dad anymore."

There were no words in me to take away the hurt. I couldn't lie to her, so I gave her a hug, rocking her back and forth in my arms. Was this the way my granddaughter's life was supposed to be?

Finally, she pulled away. "Can we make Grandpa's favorite cookies?" she asked.

"I think that's a great idea."

The next day she gave me the notice of parent/teacher conferences, as if this was the way it had always been done. Our assigned time was Friday afternoon, so I could go after Chelsea was gone with her friend.

When I entered Chelsea's homeroom on Friday, Paulette Haverbrook was sitting at her desk. About thirty-five, she was one of Chelsea's favorite teachers and I had gone to school with her mother.

I introduced myself and the woman looked confused. "Are you Chelsea's mother?" she asked. I explained the situation in as few words as possible and we discussed Chelsea's progress.

When our allotted time was almost up and I was getting ready to leave, she cleared her throat.

"Was there something else?" I asked.

"I just want to say. . . . Well, I want to say that apparently her stay with you is doing Chelsea a lot of good. I didn't realize she was no longer at home but it explains a lot of things."

"Like what?"

"Chelsea's grooming, for one thing. She's much neater and her new haircut is attractive. And she's more alert, pays better attention. She's also gained weight and she looks well cared for." She blushed. "I hope you don't mind me saying this."

"No," I said, "I don't mind. I'm happy there's at least one good side effect to all this."

When Chelsea brought her report card home the next week, she began unloading the dishwasher while I opened the envelope. I scanned the page quickly and looked up to see her watching me intently.

"How did I do, Grandma?"

I nearly laughed with delight. "You did great, sweetie," I answered. "Just great."

That's when I realized just how much I'd worried about the effect all the changes in Chelsea's life were having on her schoolwork. Apparently we were doing something right because her report card showed improvement in every area.

I quickly assembled the ingredients for Chelsea's favorite meal and we set about making a celebration dinner. Chelsea set the table while I put the chicken-and-broccoli casserole in the oven and melted some butter in a saucepan.

"What's that for, Grandma? Are you making garlic toast?"

"No, but that's a good idea." I took a loaf of sourdough bread and another stick of butter from the refrigerator. "This," I pointed to the pan on the stovetop, "is for brownies."

"Oh, I love brownies!" Chelsea said. "With nuts on top?"

I laughed. "With nuts on top." We soon had the batter mixed and spread in a pan. I gave Chelsea the chopped walnuts. "Pat these on top of the batter gently, and we'll pop the pan in the oven with the casserole."

"Oh," she said putting down the spoon she was holding. "I have a present for you, Grandma."

"What is it, sweetie?"

"I'll get it." She was out of the room and back in a flash. "Ta-dah." She held up a knitted square, slightly lopsided.

"You finished it!" I exclaimed in surprise.

"Emma's mom helped me bind it off. It's a dishcloth for you, Grandma."

"It's so pretty, I'll hate to use it," I said.

"That's okay. I can always make you another one," she said with a big grin.

I gave her a big hug. One of the wonderful benefits of having a grandchild in the house is the hugs.

By the time dinner was ready and Chelsea had summoned her grandpa from the basement, the brownies were cooling on a rack.

Al placed a small box on the table next to Chelsea's plate.

"What's that, Grandpa?"

Al sat down at the table and gave the package a doubtful look. "I don't know, sugarplum. Someone told me it's for the girl with a great report card. Is that you?"

Chelsea nodded and grinned at her grandpa.

"Then why don't you open it and see?"

Chelsea took the lid off the small box and gasped. "Oh, Grandpa!" She jumped up and threw her arms around Al's neck. "Thank you, Grandpa!" Al gave her a bear hug.

I was very curious. "What is it, sweetie?"

She held the box up and tilted it toward me. On a bed of cotton inside the box was a small, silver, heart-shaped locket. I looked over Chelsea's head at Al and raised my brows in question. He just grinned back at me. My loving, thoughtful husband is still able to surprise me.

When we'd finished eating, Chelsea got the small bowls from the cupboard while I cut the brownies. She took the ice cream from the freezer and put a scoop on each brownie. We were truly celebrating, Chelsea-style.

Chelsea's gaze kept returning to the locket next to her plate until Al offered to fasten it around her neck. She turned her back and lifted her hair from the nape of her neck as he carefully fastened the clasp before kissing the top of her head.

The sound of a car door closing interrupted the moment and signaled a change coming. Bobby appeared in the kitchen doorway.

"Daddy!" Chelsea said with delight, and then she threw her arms around Bobby's waist before leaning back and offering up the locket between two fingers. "Look at what Grandpa gave me. Isn't it beautiful?"

Bobby nodded. "Beautiful, honey." He looked around as if seeking something only he could see. "What's the occasion?"

"My report card," Chelsea said with pride. "I brought all my grades up." She twirled around in the middle of the kitchen, coming to a stop in front of me. "Could I go show Emma my new locket, please, Grandma?"

"Certainly, honey," I said. The tension in the room was escalating so fast that I could feel it like static electricity raising the hairs on my arms. "Be back in an hour, okay?"

"Okay, Grandma. 'Bye, Dad," she said, planting a kiss on Bobby's cheek.

Bobby watched her, still staring at the door after she was gone.

"Sit down, son," I finally said, sinking into my own chair.

Bobby sat and clasped his hands in front of him, staring down at them. Finally, he said, "I feel like I'm being torn into two pieces. This is the hardest thing I've ever had to do."

He rubbed his hands over his face. I'd never realized how like his dad's Bobby's habits are. Al rubbed his face the same way when he is tired. Was Bobby losing sleep? We waited.

"The counselor we've been seeing told me last night that if I want to stay married, I have to give up Chelsea."

Al snorted. "What kind of a counselor tells you to give up your own child?" he asked, his voice rough with anger.

I felt as if I were watching a landslide come down on me and I couldn't move.

Bobby shook his head. "She didn't say that, Dad. She said that in talking with us it had become clear to her that Brittany wasn't willing to bend. Oh, she talked about maturity levels and the possibility that Brittany will change someday, but what she meant was that I have to make a choice. It's Chelsea on one hand, my wife and boys on the other. Either way I lose."

My heart ached for my son and yet I understood—no, I shared— Al's anger. I stuffed it down and tried to think.

"Do you mean you want us to keep Chelsea?" I finally asked. It

88

was the only rational thought I had to hang onto: Chelsea.

Bobby nodded. "Can you—will you do that for me?"

I looked at my husband. This was a life-altering decision. It was time to decide whether we could walk the walk or just talk the talk. What did Al want? We hadn't talked about the financial aspect of raising Chelsea. Was he worried about money and how far our money would stretch? Or was he thinking of the things we might have to give up? We'd be giving up the freedom to come and go as we pleased at a moment's notice.

Al nodded just once as he looked at me and then I knew his answer. His mind hadn't changed since the night we'd first discussed this possibility. He cleared his throat. "There are some things we have to have straight between us, first," he said.

Bobby looked at his dad with hope lighting his face. "What things?"

"We'll need legal guardianship so we can make medical and legal decisions for Chelsea." Al looked at me for confirmation and I nodded before he went on. "We need to agree on some financial contribution for you to make—she is your daughter and we don't want to take that away from either one of you."

I added, "And we need to set up definite times to get the family together." At Al's puzzled look, I continued, "We don't want anyone to have hard feelings about this. We'll draw up some guidelines and we'll want Brittany to agree to them as well. Chelsea can't just be separated from the rest of her family, especially her little brothers. We'll raise Chelsea because it seems to be the best solution for everyone, but we don't want this to split up the family. Maybe this arrangement will take some pressure off Britt and we can get back to—"

"Normal?" Al prompted, and I nodded.

Bobby stood up, looking younger than he had in weeks. "I can't ever repay you," he said.

"We love you, son," Al said as he gave Bobby a hug. "Don't ever forget that."

I was sure Al was glad now that he hadn't tackled Bobby the way he wanted to when his heart was filled with anger. The more angry words that are exchanged, the harder it is to start healing.

We had our attorney draw up the guardianship papers and some guidelines and we explained to Chelsea what it would all mean. She seemed rather unimpressed. As she said, she'd planned to stay with us all along, where the love is.

I wish I could say everything was sweetness and light after that but I'd be lying. It was life—one day at a time—sometimes great and sometimes not as good. Our first get-togethers with Bobby and

Brittany were awkward, to say the least, but I think Brittany began to make a real effort when the pressure was off of her and she saw we were still willing to accept her.

Eventually we were able to have the boys for overnight visits where we watched movies together, ate popcorn, and I made chocolate malts for everybody.

Two years later I know that some clichés are true: We are never given more than we can handle. Now, instead of planning quiet fishing trips or museum tours for just the two of us, Al and I are planning slumber parties, chaperoning school dances, and attending recitals. Real retirement will come soon enough. Right now we're busy creating good memories—and I'm even finding time again to catch up on my reading.

I still see sadness in Bobby's eyes when he looks at Chelsea, but coping with his family's problems has made my son a much better man. He's a good father to all three children and maybe because of our combined attitudes, the children see their family situation as normal. In our family, it is.

THE END

GRANNY GONE BAD
I spoiled my grandkids rotten

My oldest daughter, Nicole, lived eighty miles away, which might as well have been halfway around the world for all I saw of her and my grandchildren.

She did telephone a couple of times a week, and this time she sounded excited. My grip on the telephone tightened as I anticipated what she was going to tell me. Nicole had two kids, and she'd always told me that was enough. Of course, I told her that was wrong. Children were the center of any marriage. After all my preaching, I was sure I'd finally gotten through to her. I knew she was going to tell me she was pregnant again.

"I've got great news, Mom," Nicole said. "Ray has to go to Europe to set up some computer systems for his company. He'll be there for three weeks, and I get to go with him. Isn't that wonderful? It'll be just the two of us. We haven't had a vacation in years. It'll be like a second honeymoon."

I didn't say anything for a moment. Nicole seemed to be very happy with her sudden good fortune. I was a bit disappointed. I couldn't share in the happiness of a vacation the way I could a new grandchild.

"That's wonderful news, Nicole. I'm so happy for you. It's too bad you can't take the kids, though. They'd love Europe. And I know you'll miss them."

"Are you kidding?" Nicole came back. "Those kids drive me nuts during the summer. I'll be glad to get away from them for a while."

I thought that was an awful thing to say. I knew she didn't mean it. Sometimes she let her sense of humor get out of hand.

Nicole was a good mother, in her way, and she saw to it that her kids did well in school. Still, I didn't think she paid enough attention to them. She and Ray had good jobs and could give their kids anything they wanted, yet there were plenty of things those kids had to do without. It pained me every time Nicole told them no. They had the money, so there was no reason not to give their kids what they wanted.

I was constantly telling Nicole and my other daughter, Kelly, that their kids would grow up with inferiority complexes if they weren't careful. If kids didn't have the latest toys or computer games, or the most fashionable clothes, they wouldn't be able to identify with their peers. I remember the heated argument we had four years ago over Casey's contact lenses.

"She's eight years old, Mom," Nicole had said. "She doesn't

91

need contacts. Even if she were eighteen, she wouldn't need contacts. What's wrong with glasses?"

"You know what they say: Boys don't make passes at girls who wear glasses. She'll think she's inferior. It will affect her entire life."

"Mom, Casey is a very pretty girl, and with any luck she'll grow up to be a very smart girl, too. If a boy is too dumb to see beyond a pair of glasses, then I hope Casey won't be attracted to him. She can do much better than that."

Of course, I didn't agree. Nicole was intent on making her daughters into "modern women." She wanted her girls to go to college and find good jobs and not get married until they were thirty, and maybe not even have children. That's not the kind of grandkids I wanted. The first chance I got I drove over to Gainsville and took Casey to an optometrist, where she was fitted with contact lenses. She loved them. Nicole was furious.

"Mom, I know you meant well, but you're interfering with how I raise my kids. You've gone against my wishes and I don't know how I can undo what you've done."

"You don't need to," I said. "Casey needed contacts. It's no big deal."

"Yes, it is. Now I have to keep buying contacts. She'll never wear glasses. She's got it in her head there's something wrong with glasses. She's been a bit cocky ever since she got those lenses, and her school work has suffered."

"Nicole, I don't think that's because she got contacts. Be reasonable. Her classmates have contacts, don't they?"

"I suppose," Nicole admitted. "It's her attitude I object to. I don't want you to encourage her to be a fashion model."

"I'm not," I said firmly. "I just want her to be popular. That's better than being a nerd." I'd heard the kids use that word, and I knew it was bad. My granddaughter was certainly not going to grow up to be a nerd; not when she was pretty enough to be a movie star. I couldn't understand why my daughter was so stubborn about things that seemed so simple.

It had taken Nicole months to get over that episode. And now here she was, denying her daughters the chance to go to Europe. Only there wasn't much I could do about this.

"What are you going to do with the children?" I asked. Casey was twelve now, and Susan was nine. They were certainly old enough to benefit from an extended European vacation. How would they feel about being left out? It could only have a detrimental effect on their personalities. I couldn't imagine why Nicole would even consider going off for three weeks without her kids. What was she thinking about? Certainly not her kids.

92

"We're still looking for someone to take care of them. I thought that we could send them to summer camp, but the times don't coincide. We might have to hire a nanny."

I couldn't believe my ears. She was going to be gone for three weeks, and she was perfectly willing to put her children in the hands of a stranger. What on earth was the matter with her?

"Nicole, you can't be seriously thinking about shipping your kids off someplace while you go traipsing about Europe. I know that you're a better mother than that."

I heard Nicole sigh. She always got exasperated with me when I started talking about how she raised her kids.

"Mom, the kids will be fine. We'll find someone to stay with them."

"Nonsense," I said. "You're not going to leave those kids with a stranger. They can stay here. You know we'd be happy to have them."

"Mom, I really appreciate that, but I don't think it's a good idea to have them so far away from home. All of their friends are here. There are a lot of activities they can be a part of with the people they know."

"Then I'll go there," I said firmly. "If you're going to leave your kids that long, then there should be someone you can trust to stay with them. That's what grandmothers are for." I didn't intend my remarks to sound as if Nicole were neglecting her children. Not really. But that's exactly what I thought she was doing. A woman her age, turning her back on her children just so she could have a vacation in Europe. I was ashamed to think that my daughter could be so selfish. Wally and I would certainly never have considered doing anything like that.

There was silence on the other end of the line, and I'd begun to think that we'd been cut off. Then Nicole spoke.

"I don't know, Mom. That's a long time for you to be away from home. Dad would never neglect his garden that long."

"Don't be silly. Dad wouldn't be coming. He'd just be in the way."

There was another pause, then Nicole said, "Won't Dad miss you?"

I almost laughed out loud. "Nicole, we've been married forty years. Wally wouldn't miss me if I were gone three months. He doesn't know I exist."

"Mom, that can't be true. There must be lots of things you and Dad do together."

"Do? What's to do? Without any children in the house, all we do is stare at the walls. If you'd come by more often, we'd feel a lot more useful."

"I know, Mom. It's just not that easy to get away."

What she meant was that she didn't want to give up all the things she and Ray did. The way she pushed her kids off on baby-sitters so that she could go out to a movie or dance was shameless. I couldn't understand how she and her sister had become so self-centered. I certainly hadn't raised them that way.

"Well, this time I'll be coming to you. I can use the extra bedroom, the one you don't need because you're not having any more children."

"Mom, if you come—"

"There's no if about it. You're not going to leave those poor kids with strangers for three weeks."

"Okay, okay. When you come, I don't want you spoiling the kids. Kelly told me that you spoiled her kids so badly she could barely live with them."

That was an exaggeration, of course. Kelly was my other daughter, two years younger than Nicole. She only had two kids, too. I would have had a dozen if I could, but it wasn't in the cards. Kelly and Nicole were both healthy, and they could have as many kids as they wanted. I couldn't understand why they were so selfish.

"You don't need to worry about me spoiling the kids. Or ignoring them, either."

"That's what I'm afraid of, Mom."

When I hung up, I was even more excited than Nicole had been. The prospect of spending three whole weeks with my grandchildren was better than winning the lottery. The house felt so empty once my girls had grown and moved out.

Of course, they'd been the center of our lives. Wally and I were just there to provide for them. When the girls got married, I had assumed that my house would be filled with grandchildren, but that hadn't happened. Kelly and Nicole had both been very selfish, delaying having children, and then having only two each. Nicole said she lived too far away to visit every weekend, and Kelly was always getting angry with me for "spoiling" her kids. That was nonsense.

Wally was forced into early retirement, so he didn't even have his job to keep him busy. We just sat around the house, staring at the TV. It's an awful feeling, being totally useless. Especially when you have so much to give. Sometimes I had this wonderful dream where I moved in with Nicole and Wally moved in with Kelly. Then we could always be with the grandkids.

The grandkids needed us around, too. To be honest, Nicole and Kelly did all they could for their children. But there were plenty of times they had put their kids in the background so that they could do something themselves. They were so self-centered that I was often embarrassed to call them my children. Take Nicole, for instance. I

94

couldn't imagine how she could abandon her kids for three whole weeks.

Every cloud has its silver lining, though, and I would get to spend those three weeks with my grandkids. I'd feel like a mother again, with children to care for and love. I'd feel useful again.

I burst into the living room to tell Wally the good news. He had the TV on and the newspaper was hiding his face. He didn't put the paper down when I began talking to him. All he said was, "That's nice." At least, I think that's what he said. He was mumbling, and with the TV on, I couldn't really hear what he said.

A few weeks later, I packed my suitcase and made the hour and a half drive to Gainsville. Nicole lived in a nice two-storey house with a big yard. It was the perfect place to raise kids. It was too bad there were only two of them.

Casey and Susan ran into the driveway and threw their arms around me almost before I could get out of the car. The poor things. They were obviously starved for affection. I only had three weeks to make up for years of neglect, but I would do my best.

"We'll carry your bags in, Grandma," Susan said, struggling with a suitcase that was bigger than her.

"You'll do no such thing," I said firmly. "Children shouldn't be workhorses. You just hold the door open and your father and I will bring these things in."

Casey was already at the front door with two of my bags, and Susan had picked up a smaller bag and followed her, squealing with delight all the way. I sighed heavily. I obviously had my work cut out for me.

I got settled into the big spare bedroom that would've been perfect for a little baby. One day, when it was too late, Nicole's kids would be grown and she'd find herself lost in an empty house. Then she'd wish she had more children.

Ray and Nicole both gave me instructions before they left. I didn't pay too much attention. Neither one of them seemed to think I knew how to handle children. I could've told them that I knew a lot more about it than they did, but I didn't want to start an argument. The sooner they left, the sooner I could get started doing my job—being a mother. I mean, being a grandmother.

That first day alone with the kids was an eye-opener. I'd had trouble getting to sleep, probably because it was a strange bed, and so I overslept. I didn't stir until I smelled food cooking.

Getting dressed and scurrying downstairs, I was horrified to find Casey and Susan in the kitchen. They had breakfast all cooked and the breakfast table set.

"We were going to bring you up a tray," Susan said brightly, as she placed a third setting at the table.

"Oh, heavens, I'm so sorry. You shouldn't be doing any of this."

"We cook all the time," Casey said. "It's a big help to Mom."

"I guess so," I said indignantly. She made these poor kids work so that she could have a job and buy fancy clothes and a nice car. If she had any decency, she'd stay home and take care of her kids, like a mother should.

I made them sit down and took over. After we finished eating, I started clearing the table. The girls pitched right in, until I put a stop to it.

"But, Grandma, we wash dishes all the time," Susan said. "It's part of our chores."

"Chores! Children shouldn't have chores in this day and age. You'd think we were living in the dark ages. You two run along. Go play or watch TV."

They both stared at me with a bewildered look on their faces.

"We're only allowed to watch two hours of television a day, and never before supper," Susan said, with a look so serious it made me want to cry.

"You poor children. You're not being allowed to have a childhood."

"What?" Casey asked.

"Oh, never mind. You two go on and do whatever you want. For the next three weeks, you're on vacation. I don't want to see you do any work at all. Not as long as I'm here."

"Great," Susan said. Casey was more hesitant.

"I'm supposed to mow the grass today, Grandma."

I nearly dropped a plate on the floor. "You mean that your mother makes you mow this big yard with that dangerous power mower? That's positively shameful, and I won't have any of it. I'll take care of all the chores, including the grass."

"But, Grandma—"

"I've heard enough. Now you two run along."

I was truly hurt to learn that my own daughter was such a bad mother. The very idea of making her kids do housework and yard work was appalling. And in the summer, no less, when they should be out playing and having fun. I'd certainly never raised my children like that. I did all the housework so that they could enjoy their childhood. You only had it once. When Nicole got back from Europe I'd have a stern talk with her.

The girls just didn't know what to do with themselves. I finally gave them fifty dollars and told them to go to the mall. That's what young people like to do nowadays. And I told them they didn't have to be back until evening. They'd probably like eating a hot dog at the mall.

"Mom says that's junk food," Susan said. "She doesn't like us to eat junk food."

"My heavens, what a miserable life you girls have. You like hot dogs, don't you?"

"I guess so," Susan said, looking to Casey for support.

"Then you can have hot dogs. I ate plenty of them when I was a child, and they never hurt me. And tomorrow we'll go to the store and stock up on potato chips and other snacks. You don't have any in the entire house."

The girls took off with a gleam in their eyes. I could tell that, probably for the first time, they were enjoying themselves.

After I did the dishes, I did a little dusting, and then I tackled the mowing job. By the time I got half way through, I was exhausted. With a yard that big, they really needed a riding mower. Making Casey do that kind of work was inhumane. Probably illegal, too.

When I finished the yard, I went inside and collapsed on the sofa. I didn't even think about the rest of the housework. I drifted off to sleep and didn't wake until the kids came home at about six o'clock.

"We'll start supper, Grandma. You rest up."

"You'll do no such thing," I said, sitting up and wincing at my sore muscles. I didn't think I had the energy to go into the kitchen and fix anything. "Why don't we order pizza? That sounds like a good idea, doesn't it?" I asked the girls.

They were delighted. That night I let them watch TV until way past their bedtime, and I let them drink as much soda as they wanted. The idea of putting a limit on their soft drinks was preposterous. If only Nicole would let me see more of the kids, I'd change more than a thing or two.

The next day was Sunday, and we drove to the grocery store and stocked up on chips, pretzels, dip, soda, ice cream, candy, popcorn and, of course, hot dogs. Then we stopped at a video store and rented some movies and video games.

"This is great, Grandma," Susan said later as she stuffed herself with hot dogs and ice cream in front of the TV. "Mom doesn't let us do anything like this."

"Well, it's a crying shame, that's all I can say."

Susan was sick that night, so I let her sleep with me. Of course, I didn't get much rest because I had to keep her entertained until she settled down, and I was tired the next morning. That's when I got another big surprise. Casey told me she had to be in summer school by ten o'clock. Nicole had signed her up for a four-week algebra class, if you can believe that. I didn't remember Nicole or Ray saying a thing about it.

"Why on earth do you want to go to summer school?" I

demanded. "And algebra, no less. You won't need to know any of that. Certainly not at twelve."

"Mom thought it was a good idea," Casey said. "She wanted me to get a head start in mathematics."

"You need to take homemaking classes," I said. "One of these days you'll be a mother yourself, and you'll need to know how to keep a house."

I had turned away from them, but from the corner of my eye I saw Casey conceal a laugh with her hand. Girls always laughed when you talked about babies.

I got hold of the school and explained that there had been a change of plans, and that Casey would not be attending summer school. Certainly not for an algebra class. Summers were for fun, not schoolwork. Nicole should know that better than anyone. I never forced her to go to summer school.

It didn't take long for the kids to start acting like kids. They quickly got used to staying up late, sleeping late, spoiling their appetites with candy, having parties, making messes, and above all, shopping at the mall. Whenever they wanted to go, I gave them plenty of money to spend.

The whole time they were gone, Ray and Nicole only called a few times. They probably weren't thinking about their kids at all. This younger generation was so selfish. I warned the girls not to say anything about their new life-style when they were on the phone with their parents. What Nicole didn't know wouldn't hurt her.

The three weeks went by all too soon, and the kids had tears in their eyes when they kissed me good-bye.

"We'll miss you, Grandma," Susan said.

"And I'll miss you, too," I said, fighting back my own tears. I knew that as soon as I pulled out of the driveway, Nicole would be putting the kids to work. The idea was so awful I didn't like to think about it. Nicole should be doing for them. That's what mothers were for.

The next afternoon Nicole telephoned me. She was so angry I barely recognized her voice.

"What have you done to my kids? I can't get them to do anything anymore. I've been fighting with them ever since you left."

I couldn't imagine what she was talking about. "I didn't have a bit of trouble with them, Nicole. Maybe you expect too much of them. Why don't you just let them be kids? If you quit your fancy job and stayed home you'd have time to do for your kids."

I heard a sharp intake of breath. Maybe I had stepped over the line, but somebody had to tell Nicole what she was doing was wrong.

"It's not a question of me having time," Nicole said, her voice sounding strained, as if she were trying to keep it under control. "I'm talking about teaching the children discipline and responsibility. How to manage money. How to eat properly. The importance of a good education. Now all they think about is fun and games, and begging me for money so that they can squander it away at the mall."

"Children shouldn't have to think about anything but fun and games. And you can certainly afford to give the girls spending money."

"You're not listening, are you? You don't understand anything I've been saying."

"I know how to raise kids," I said. "You need to pay more attention to those precious things."

"You've turned those precious things into little monsters. In only three weeks you've destroyed all Ray and I have accomplished."

"If those were my kids—"

"They're not, Mom. They're mine, and I'm tired of you interfering in their lives. You've done enough damage to last a lifetime. I should've known better than to let you stay here with them. I should've listened to Kelly. You've spoiled her kids rotten."

"Now, just a minute, Nicole—"

"You're not going to have any more extended visits with my kids, Mom. You're ruining them."

"You can't mean that, Nicole." She was just angry and over-reacting. She wouldn't keep the grandchildren away from me. She wouldn't do that to her own mother, would she?

"I do mean it, Mom. We'll come by and visit a few hours, and that's it. No more overnighters. No more weekends. I'm tired of you destroying everything I've worked so hard to accomplish. You interfere too much and it has to stop. Kelly won't stand up to you, but I will."

I started to choke up. She was taking the kids away from me! That wasn't fair.

"Nicole, I've never interfered and you know it. I'm only being what I am—a mother. You can't hold that against me."

"You're corrupting my children. That's interference enough. Why don't you get a life?"

"What? Get a life! What on earth do you mean? Your kids are my life. Yours and Kelly's. That's what I live for. I just want to be a mother, I mean a grandmother, to them."

"Don't you and Dad ever do anything?" Nicole asked unexpectedly. "Don't you go out once in a while, take in a movie, just go for a walk and hold hands?"

Even though I was upset, I couldn't help laughing. The notion of Wally and me holding hands was so preposterous. "Nicole, your father and I have been married—"

"I know. Forty years. But that doesn't matter if you still love each other. Ray and I don't have the same priorities that you do. Children aren't the center of our lives."

"Oh, Nicole, how can you say such a thing? I know you love those adorable girls."

"Yes," she came back promptly, "I do love them. And they should be taught to be responsible adults, because one day they will go out on their own. And when that happens, this house will be a lot quieter. But it won't be empty, like yours. That's because Ray is the center of my life, and I'm the center of his. Ray and I will always have each other. All you've got is an empty house. I feel sorry for you, Mom, but I'm not about to allow you to spoil my children. They have to learn to be responsible, and to develop their own personalities. I wouldn't want them to grow up to have empty lives like yours."

Then there was a loud click. I stood there for a long moment with the phone in my hand. Nicole had never talked to me like that before, and it hurt me to my very bones. She surely couldn't mean half the things she'd said. Wouldn't her children resent her when they were grown? She would have nothing then, except her husband. And she'd soon find that was almost nothing. I mean, Wally and I hadn't really been close for years. For decades, really. We'd put our children first, as was proper. Wasn't it?

I began to wonder. My life certainly was empty without kids running around. And I knew plenty of women whose children lived thousands of miles away—they seldom saw their grandkids. I'd always thought that I was lucky because my grandkids weren't that far away. But my own children seemed to disapprove of what I tried to do for the grandkids. It didn't make sense to me.

A few hours later Wally came home. I had no idea where he'd been, although I'm sure he'd mentioned it. I hadn't paid attention because it hadn't mattered much. Wally never did anything important. Only this time he had.

"I was at the doctor's," he explained when I asked where he had been. "He had the results from my tests."

Tests? I didn't remember Wally having any tests done. Had I been ignoring him that much?

"You're okay, aren't you?" I asked.

"Sure," he said. "It was a false positive the first time. Nothing to worry about."

Of course I hadn't worried. I hadn't even known. He had, long ago, become little more than a roommate to me. That's certainly not how we had begun our relationship. At one time we had been passionate lovers. I'd had to fight him off until we were married. Then the kids came and things changed. I forgot all about Wally, and he forgot about me.

Our children became the focus of our lives, and Wally and I lost touch with each other. Then the kids grew up and we had nothing but each other. By that point we felt like strangers. We didn't even talk. That couldn't be right, could it? Not after all that we had once had together. What had gone wrong?

Wally and I weren't rich, but we had plenty of money for our needs. We should've had a lot going for us. Why didn't we? All I had was the grandkids, and all Wally had was, well, he had the grandkids, too, I suppose. What was obvious was that we didn't have each other, and hadn't for quite some time. Yet we'd once been deeply in love. Something had gone wrong somewhere, although I couldn't put my finger on the precise moment.

Nicole and Kelly both seemed to think I was a meddler. Maybe there was something to what they said. They did seem to have lives of their own, while all I had were memories of a life once lived. Maybe there was life still to be lived. I'd never thought that before, and now the idea seemed quite thrilling.

I didn't even know how to start. I began by paying more attention to how I looked. Just because Wally was the only one around was no excuse to be sloppy. Although I had gained a few pounds over the years, I still had the curves of a woman. I had just been hiding them under shapeless clothes, because once it became obvious I could no longer get pregnant there didn't seem to be any reason for Wally and me to sleep together.

Now I wasn't so sure. There had been plenty of times I had wanted him in my bed, wanted him as much as when I had been twenty. Only, after the kids were grown, it didn't seem right. I had transferred my love for Wally to my own children, and that wasn't fair. Wally was the man I had married, and he deserved my love and affection.

It was a long and slow process to regain my life with Wally. We began doing things together—little things, like working in the garden or shopping. We started taking walks in the afternoon, and I always held his hand. We discovered that we liked being together.

About a year later, we bought a motor home and started taking trips. One night we were parked by a lake, and there wasn't another soul around. Under a full moon, Wally and I made love for the first time in more than a decade. That's when I realized that we had finally rediscovered each other. Our lives stopped being empty because we realized we had each other. All those years, we had lived like disinterested roommates, yet somehow we were able to rekindle the love we had originally.

At long last, we discovered the most important thing in our lives was each other. Children will grow up and eventually find their own loves, and their parents will have nothing but each other. If they'd built their lives around their children, then they'll have nothing when the children leave. Wally and I were lucky. Our love had been dormant for decades, but it was strong enough that it could be revived.

I long ago patched things up with Kelly and Nicole. I came around to their way of thinking—that children should be taught good habits and responsibility. Now I don't spoil the grandkids—I participate in their upbringing. Kelly and Nicole don't hesitate to call me now to be a baby-sitter. Wally and I are happy to do that whenever we can, but we're not always available. We have our own lives to live now.

I married Wally because I loved him. After forty years of marriage, I'm thrilled to say that I still love him.

THE END

GOING TO GRANDMA'S
A reader shares her special weekend with
her very accident-prone grandson!

"Here I am, Mam-ma."
My youngest grandson, Hunter, was staying with me overnight while his parents and older brother, Aiden, made a trip to see an eye specialist for Aiden. Hunter brought in his favorite blanket and his little bag that had Going To Grandma's printed on it and headed for the TV in the den. Hunter always commandeered the den TV because it has a VCR and he usually brings some movies, too.

His parents and brother left in a hurry, thinking Hunter might fuss a little. Of course he didn't. He was eight years old—a big boy— and loved it at my house for some unknown reason. I guess cable TV, being able to sit in the den, and eating and drinking on a towel might've had something to do with it. He might get bored before his parents returned, but he was happy for the time being.

I asked Hunter what he wanted for supper and spaghetti was chosen. I had a few qualms, but spaghetti it was. Hunter knocked over one soda, spilled spaghetti three times, and after he had chocolate ice cream for dessert, the bathroom was a mess.

I was aghast when I went in. My pale yellow bathroom had chocolate spots everywhere! How do children do this? I just shook my head. Hunter must've half-washed, then flung his hands to get the water off—well, not all the water. I noticed my yellow towels had brown spots, too.

Well, he'll be gone tomorrow afternoon and then I can clean up.

The next day, I was groggy from lack of sleep. I had to sleep with Hunter in the spare room. He still wasn't sleeping alone and usually slept with his brother. But when Hunter sailed out of the house after breakfast, I breathed a little easier.

A scream from outside set my ears on edge. "Mam-ma, Mam-ma, come quick!"

What now? He sounded like someone had cut his hands off.

He came running up, dancing around and slinging his hands.

"Ow! Ow! Do something, Mam-ma!"

Hunter had fallen into a bed of fire ants! I stripped him down and doctored the bites, which were not nearly as many as I first thought. He was allergic to bites, though, but I had his medication. He was back outside in a half-hour.

"Be careful, please. No more ants."

103

Hunter grinned and took off on his bike. I went back to my work.

I heard another scream and then dreadful crying. I ran to the door and Hunter was in the driveway, tangled up in his bike. His foot was caught in the spokes and he had skinned knees and elbows.

I ran outside and untangled the shrieking child. He could always get a part in a horror movie.

"Oh, my. You've got some bad abrasions there, Hunter. We'll have to put some medicine on them!"

"No, no! It'll burn, it'll burn!" he cried. "Mam-ma, what's a 'brasion?"

"A boo-boo, a skinned place." I finally talked him into doctoring the boo-boos. "Hunter, you have to slow down a little. I'm not used to little boys getting hurt every five minutes."

He sniffled for a while, and then got up again.

"Hunter, you can't get back on the bike. Your dad or Pap-pa will have to straighten the spokes!" I yelled as he banged out the back door.

Everything went smoothly for maybe an hour. I looked outside and didn't see or hear him. And then suddenly, a little head appeared, coming up the hill behind our house. The hair looked a little wet, the clothes a little awry.

When he saw me, he hurried a little.

Uh, oh, I thought. He and the creek had a little run-in.

"I'm sorry, Mam-ma. I fell in the creek."

"And why did you fall in the creek?"

"I tried to cross the old log and . . . and—"

"Slipped off? And how many times has Pap-pa told you to stay off that log? Come on; let's get a bath and clean clothes. Your parents will be here in about two hours."

"But I'm not ready to go home!"

"Hunter, you'll have to go home tonight, sweetheart. Mam-ma has an appointment tomorrow."

"Shoot," he said and frowned, then repeated what he heard his mom and brother say. "Your 'pointments get in my way."

I laughed, started the water in the tub, and then gave the little fellow a good bath and clean clothes. We were having a snack when his folks came.

"Were you a good boy?" My daughter's eyebrows went up when she saw the bruises, scrapes, and the swollen ant bites.

"Hunter, what on earth did you do?"

"Well, fire ants got me, I had a bike wreck, I fell in the creek, and I musta done something in the bathroom because I saw Mam-ma scrubbing in there."

I looked at my daughter and mouthed the word: chocolate.

"Ready to go, boy?" His dad picked up his suitcase and off they went.

"I'll be back soon as you have time, Mam-ma."

"Mam-ma probably won't want to see you for a while," said his fourteen-year-old brother, Aiden.

Hunter just gave him a nasty look. "Why not?"

They all left and I plopped down in a chair. My husband came in and grinned. "Boy, this has been a real doozy of a 'granny-do' day, hasn't it?"

I gave him a Don't even start look.

I was busy for the next few days and then Mother's Day came up, so the children all would be over sometime that day.

My son and younger daughter live next door and they brought me pretty cards and a lovely plaque, and then Hunter and Aiden came with their dad. Their mother came down with a virus and she sent her gift along with the boys.

Aiden came in with the gift from his mother—a lovely angel pin. Hunter came up shyly at first and then he handed me a card.

"This is from Aiden and me."

I took the card and opened it. It was a cute card with the Count from Sesame Street on the front.

"Hunter picked it out, Mam-ma," Aiden said, and grinned.

Hunter was still standing in front of me as he pulled a small sack from behind his back suddenly and handed it to me.

"And this is from just me."

I opened the little sack and found two heart-shaped, lilac bath oil beads inside. Hunter picked them out himself at the drugstore.

I hugged Hunter and thanked him profusely. The spaghetti, the chocolate, the accidents, and the sleepless night went right out the window, as it would with any grandmother. That little sack with the bath oil beads, those beautiful eyes smiling up at me, and my grandson saying from just me was the total epitome for me of the joy of being a grandmother.

Hunter's mother told me later that he wanted her to say it for him. He was too bashful, but he came through with flying colors. I will always remember this and will certainly retell it when he's a grown man—how it brightened up a grandma's day to get a present from Just Me.

THE END

GRANDMAS—GOD'S ANGELS IN DISGUISE

True Story salutes a reader's sweet wisdom— and loving sacrifice

The phone rang and my teenage granddaughter's tearful voice cried, "Grandma! Can you come get me from drill practice? I don't have a ride home!"

I glanced at the timer on the stove; my cake still had twenty minutes to bake, but from the sound of Hayley's frantic appeal, I decided I'd better leave right then and go pick her up. Apparently, my new daughter-in-law, Tina, Hayley's stepmother, had forgotten her again and wasn't answering her cell phone. I knew I couldn't risk leaving my precious granddaughter stranded at a deserted school gymnasium in today's world. No telling what might happen.

"Be right there, honey. Watch for me out front."

I turned the oven down, hoping to be back before the cake was ruined. Grabbing my purse and car keys, I headed for the door. A quick glance in the hall mirror stopped me long enough to brush flour from my nose and smooth my gray hair.

Hayley waved to me when I parked outside the building. She wasn't alone, as I'd feared, but rather, was in the midst of a cluster of girls dressed in red-and-white drill-team uniforms. I waited impatiently, eyeing my wristwatch, then tooted the horn when she went on chatting just as though I wasn't there, waiting for her.

"Hello, dear," I greeted as she slid into the passenger seat. "I thought you were in a hurry; I left a cake baking in the oven to come get you, you know."

"A cake! Yummy! I'm starved!" She didn't sound the least bit tearful; in fact, she was definitely in high spirits.

"Where's Tina?" I asked, putting the car in gear. I still couldn't bring myself to refer to Andy's new wife to Hayley as "your mother." As it was, Tina, the newest addition to our family, seemed little more than a child herself—and certainly seemed entirely incapable of helping to raise three children!

"Gee, I don't know," Hayley replied.

"You didn't call her?"

Hayley shook her head. "I only had enough change for one phone call, Grandma. I called you because I knew you'd be home."

The slight irritation I felt quickly dissolved in light of the trust my granddaughter placed in me. As it was, I'd become a substitute mom to Hayley and her siblings, Braylen and Sara, when their real mom decided she wanted to break things off with Andy and devote her time to her lesbian girlfriend.

"Well, then—I'll just run you home after we check on my cake," I told her.

When we pulled into the driveway a pleasant aroma wafted out to us through the open kitchen window.

"Mmmm. German chocolate, Grandma?" Hayley asked. It's her favorite, and her father's, too. "Can I have a piece while it's still hot?"

The sweetheart. Her brown eyes sparkled with anticipation. "Of course, dear." How I hoped I'd always be able to provide treats for my grandchildren and be there for them whenever they needed me.

We shared cake and milk companionably at the kitchen counter while Hayley chattered nonstop about school, boys, and drill team. The ringing of the phone startled us both about an hour later.

"Myrna? Is Hayley there?"

"Yes, she is." It's Tina, I silently mouthed as I handed the phone to Hayley.

While she listened and murmured, "Um, okay," and "Uh-huh," I watched my granddaughter closely. Her apparent agitation increased as she talked, and my heart wrenched. More conflict at home, it seemed. Would it never end? Finally, she replaced the receiver and laid her head on her arm on the kitchen counter.

I lifted her chin to reveal moisture-dampened mascara. "What is it, Hayley, precious?"

"She's mad at me again. She's always mad at me." Her youthful chin quivered. "I was supposed to go home and stay with Sara while she took Braylen to the dentist, I guess."

"But didn't she know about drill practice? How could you be both places at once?"

"That's what I'd like to know!" The small, pointed chin stopped quivering and jutted defiantly. "She expects too much. Why can't she just leave me alone, Grandma?"

"There, there, honey. It's okay, dear," I soothed. "Dry your eyes and we'll go. You can finish your cake on the way."

"I wish I didn't have to go. I wish I lived here with you instead of with her, Grandma."

Me, too, I thought, but I held my tongue. I hated taking Hayley home to be reprimanded—and probably punished because of a simple lack of communication. I wanted to wrap her and my other grandchildren safely in my arms and keep them forever from heartache and unhappiness at the mercy of their new stepmother.

Oh, not that Tina was mean or abusive. Grudgingly, I have to admit she can be nice when she wants to. As it was, though, she was just too strict with her stepchildren. To my way of thinking, her ideas of discipline were those of an Army drill sergeant! I worried that she would crush their sweet, bubbly, boisterous, wonderful spirits.

The sudden abandonment by their mother was adjustment enough, making them timid and afraid. As it was, I was sure that each of them thought they were personally responsible for their mom leaving, since that's the way kids reason. Sara was only six, Braylen ten, and Hayley thirteen when Eileen left. With Andy's dazed approval, I brought them home to stay with me for a while where I could wipe their tears and kiss away their hurts. They watched out the window for days, hoping against hope that their mother would return to them. All I could do was smooth the surfaces and try my hardest to make them feel safe and secure. I played games with them, took them on tours, baked their favorite goodies and cooked their favorite meals, and gave them a lap to sit in and shoulders to cry on. Eventually, their natural childish and adolescent exuberance began to emerge again. With the sunny environment I provided, the terrible clouds began to dissipate and drift away.

I tried to reach out to my son, Andy, too, but he held himself aloof. The gap between us grew wider and wider and after awhile he seemed so lost and bewildered, but when I tried to comfort him, he pushed me away. It broke my heart, but how could I help him when I didn't understand Eileen's betrayal any more than he did?

We both meant for the children's stay to be temporary, but after awhile, the pattern of having them at my house while Andy worked— and recovered—became established and the days turned into weeks, then months. We all became content with these arrangements— especially me, I admit. I'll even admit that I doted on my grandchildren as I never had my son when he was little. Therefore, when Andy finally started dating again, I had natural reservations, even though I know men aren't meant to live alone.

The first time he brought Tina home to meet the children and me, I was apprehensive and nervous. He called earlier to prepare us, but I was scarcely prepared for the seriousness of their altogether new "relationship." As I watched them throughout that first fateful evening, it shocked me to even think of this flesh-and-blood woman becoming a "replacement" for my former daughter-in-law. Tina's certainly pretty enough, but she was so young—only ten years older than Hayley, in fact!

After a rather awkward conversation during dinner, interrupted by an occasional cut-up by Braylen, who's a natural clown, I couldn't actually fault the soft-spoken, gentle-mannered young woman sitting next to Andy, but neither could I relax in her presence. It was almost as though I sensed how stubborn and regimental she'd become once she married my son.

In the days that followed, I seldom got to observe firsthand her treatment of my grandchildren, but they were constantly telling me how fussy and particular she was, and how she put them through their paces. More than once they came to my house crying because of conflicts at home and it certainly seemed to me that nothing they did pleased their new stepmother.

Oh, well, I thought as I cleaned up the crumbs from the counter after driving Hayley home, all I can do is be here when my grandchildren need me. I whipped up a coconut-pecan frosting for the remainder of the cake, all the while wondering why I even bothered. With the kids gone, the cake would probably sit and mold, then ultimately end up in the garbage. With the kids gone, the effort of making desserts was too often a big waste of time . . . as were the majority of my sterile, empty days.

Oh, well, I thought again with a sigh. At least Hayley enjoyed one of her grandma's special treats!

Hayley. The memory of her stricken face when I dropped her off haunted me the rest of that afternoon as I wondered, How did she fare in her confrontation with Tina? Several times I picked up the phone to call, then, in the process of dialing, realized the matter was out of my hands. Knowing Tina's policy that "the punishment should fit the crime," I wondered how severely my granddaughter would be treated for something as simple as forgetting a babysitting commitment. Will Tina pull her off the drill team? Or will drill practice prove to be a mitigating circumstance? It was hard to tell with my daughter-in-law, who was also prosecutor, judge, and jury.

When Andy stopped by after work to repair a broken lawn sprinkler, I met him at the door and explained what happened.

"I hope Tina will go easy on Hayley," I told him. "Teenagers are under enough pressure these days without getting more at home."

Andy had his back to me, but I saw his neck muscles tighten. Well, I thought, but dared not say, if you'd intervene once in a while your wife might lighten up a bit. Something needs to be done. She's making martinets of my once well-adjusted grandchildren!

For instance, just last week Braylen caught the brunt of her anger. "For sassing," he told me with a grimace while he sat beside me on my couch and explained what happened. "But I didn't sass her, Grandma. Honest! When she told me I couldn't watch TV until my homework was done, I just tried to tell her that I can do both at the same time."

What is the matter with that woman? I wondered then fretfully. Of course Braylen can study and watch TV at the same time; he certainly does it at my house all the time. Besides, he isn't the sassing type. He's never been smart-mouthed with me—that's for certain! Tina's simply too young to recognize the difference between talking back and sticking up for oneself.

"Then what happened, Braylen?" I quizzed him.

His small face puckered up as he remembered. "She took away my TV privileges for a week—'Until you learn some manners, young man.'"

Rather harsh punishment for a ten-year-old, I'd say. To make up for Tina's unreasonableness I thought about suggesting that she let Braylen come to my house to do his homework. But the more I pondered it, the more I decided maybe that wasn't such a good idea. After all, I didn't want to cause more trouble between the two of them. Instead, I took him to Dairy Queen for a banana split. At that point, I figured all I could do was offer a rainbow after the storm.

Even little Sara needed a buffer to guard her against her "new mother". The delightful first-grader never clashed with anyone in her young life . . . until Tina came along. Easygoing and always willing to please, her joyous spirit always put Sara in good stead with everyone around her, but Tina harped on her over the least little things: Don't chew on your hair; tie your own shoes; chew with your mouth closed; don't pick your nose; clean up your toys—just to name a few. Small, insignificant things that all children are often guilty of, but shouldn't be called to task for so much so that it impedes their natural development.

Often, I went to pick Sara up after school so she could have playtime instead of being a marionette, with Tina pulling her strings. Her complaints were small compared to Braylen's and Hayley's, but I could tell she resented the strict rules she was obliged to live by under her stepmother's jurisdiction.

If only Tina could see the damage she's causing by overcorrecting the children, I fretted almost constantly. As it is, they're changing from cheerful, happy, bright individuals into resentful, morose, young robots.

I tried to talk to Andy about her after work when he stopped by to repair that broken sprinkler I'd called about earlier; I met him at the door and explained to him what'd happened with Hayley. The whole time he resolutely kept his back turned and twisted on the broken sprinkler, clamming up like a fresh-sealed bottle of preserves. I could see by the set of his jaw that I'd get no help from him.

"I hope Tina will go easy on Hayley; I know it's not my place to speak to Tina," I told him, wringing my hands anxiously. "She'll only consider me an interfering mother-in-law. But if worse comes to worse, I will. Someone has to, after all—for the children's sakes."

We'd had this conversation before—many times, in fact—and always with the same results: silence and hostility. After awhile, my son finally muttered something under his breath.

"What was that, Andy? Speak up, please. You know I'm getting a little hard of hearing these days."

He slowly turned to face me, giving me a pained look. "Tina's doing her best, Mom. Just once, won't you at least please give her the benefit of the doubt?"

***In all fairness, I did try during the days that followed, but I honestly felt like I could do a better job of disciplining my grandchildren with my hands tied behind my back! And yet I stood by helplessly and watched my beautiful grandchildren become increasingly sullen and uncooperative. Even my happy-go-lucky Sara started bursting into tears at the slightest provocation, and after awhile, my telephone quit ringing off the hook with pleas from Hayley, and Braylen stopped telling me about his latest run-ins with Tina—

And I quit getting last-minute calls asking me to babysit Sara.

Listless with inactivity, I no longer filled my kitchen with the tempting aromas of baked goods. After all, I decided, why should I when my grandchildren seldom come over to visit? Board games no longer littered my living room coffee table, and the TV remained off for days on end. The nights were excruciatingly monotonous; I vegetated, worrying nonstop about what was happening at my son's house. I even stooped to spying on their neighborhood from a safe distance and checking at school to see if, by chance, my grandchildren were being left stranded at the curb. But my brief glimpses of them getting in and out of Tina's Suburban and dragging their feet up the sidewalk to their house revealed only that they seemed sad and disconsolate.

On the rare occasions when I had the family over for dinner or attended one of the children's school functions, my precious darlings were guarded like prisoners. I observed with dismay how a simple lift of an eyebrow or a clearing of the throat would stifle the most exuberant outburst. Their manners were impeccable—and suspiciously unnatural for children their ages—even little Sara, who appeared near tears most of the time.

Obviously, my seemingly gentle daughter-in-law was an ogre at home. But when I tried to quiz my son about her behavior, Andy always sided with her, inferring in an offhand way that I was a busybody.

Me, his own mother!

I indulged my unhappiness with shopping binges for my grandchildren. Sparing no expense, I bought them the latest fashions—piled bags of clothing, makeup, and perfume for Hayley, electronic games for Braylen, and Barbie dolls for Sara and packed them into my car the next time I went to visit. Andy returned most of my purchases a day or two later with the price tags still intact.

"What in the world?" I sputtered. "Can't I even buy gifts for my grandchildren?"

"Tina says you're being too generous, Mom. She thinks the kids will learn to appreciate things more if they earn them." He ducked his head, but I could swear that, instead of seeming embarrassed, he was actually suppressing a smile!

"That's ridiculous, Andrew George! I am their grandmother, for Pete's sake! And that—that woman—" I caught myself before I spewed out what I really thought of Tina. From past experience, I knew the truth would only alienate my son from me.

"Listen, Mom—save them for Christmas if you want," he suggested, reverting to being the diplomat he's always been by nature. "I'm sure your grandkids will be positively thrilled to find all those wonderful surprises under the tree."

"Christmas? But these are summer things, Andrew. And the holidays are still months away! The way they're growing, the clothes won't even fit them anymore come Christmastime!"

As it was, I wasn't looking forward to Christ's birthday the way I usually do. Nothing would be the same, I was sure—no rollicking trip to the hills for a Christmas tree, no making snow angels or throwing snowballs, no chopping down the perfect tree (which always turned out to be the most lopsided), no impromptu caroling, young bodies bundled in warm clothes and earmuffs, breath foggy in the December air. No cookie making, with more cookies consumed than saved. No surprises. Knowing Tina, I'd decided that Christmas would probably be stark and bleak.

I snatched the bags from Andy. "Oh, just forget it, then! I'll return everything myself—if the stores will let me!"

Disappointed that my last-ditch effort at being a grandmother had failed, I resigned myself to the inevitable and swore I'd stay home and mind my own business and let my son find out for himself just how miserable his new wife was making his children.

Listless with inactivity, I quit filling my kitchen with tempting aromas of home-baked goods, put the board games away in the back of the hall closet, cleaned up the clutter of paper airplanes, crayons, coloring books, and Barbies from the family room, and put all the children's books back on the shelves. The TV stayed off for days on end and my nights became excruciatingly lonely and monotonous.

I vegetated, worrying nonstop about what was happening at my son's house. Even on the precious occasions when I had the family over for Sunday dinner or attended one of the children's school functions, my precious darlings were guarded like virtual prisoners.

Then one day, shortly after the kids started back at school, I got a call from Braylen's principal.

"Mrs. Thomas? Can you come to the school, please? Right away? I can't seem to get in touch with Braylen's parents and we have a problem here. You are Braylen's grandmother, aren't you?"

"That's right." I swelled with pride. Surely, Mr. Weston hadn't forgotten my past visits to the school. Still, he sounded a little uncomfortable on the phone, like maybe Tina had given him orders not to call me. "What is it? Is Braylen all right?"

"Braylen's fine, but—" He coughed. "I'll tell you about it when you get here. You wouldn't happen to know how to contact his parents, would you?"

"Er, no." I had both Andy's and Tina's unlisted cell phone numbers memorized in case of an emergency, but it didn't sound as though this was anything I couldn't handle. After all, I thought, didn't I always stay on top of things when I was in charge? Still, my heart began to pound. "I'll be at the school in five minutes," I told the principal, reaching for my car keys.

Hayley met me outside the school building. She was white as a sheet. "Grandma, I think Braylen's in big trouble."

That's when I noticed that a police cruiser was parked at the curb. Clusters of curious onlookers watched in hushed silence as we approached.

"Hayley! What are you doing here?" The middle school she attended was three blocks away.

"My school lets out early on Wednesdays, and I came to meet Braylen and Sara so we can ride home together."

Came to keep Braylen from the Big Bad Wolf, she meant. I was grateful for my precious granddaughter's mature concern for her younger brother.

"What happened?" I asked. Mr. Weston had been so vague. If Hayley knew anything, I wanted her to fill me in so I'd be prepared. I reached for her hands and found they were as cold as ice.

"What I was told. . . ." she began after taking a deep breath, ". . . .is that Braylen and his friends dared each other to put the sixth-grade class's pet boa constrictor in with their fourth-grade teacher's pet mice."

"Oh. Is that all?" The fist that had been gripping my stomach relaxed and I felt a laugh bubbling up inside of me. It certainly sounded like something Braylen would do; he can be so impulsive at times. "But why are the police here?"

"Well, um . . . I guess Braylen's teacher, Miss Beckstead, came back early from a staff meeting or something and heard the boys giggling. When she saw the long, green snake in the mice's cage with several lumps in its stomach, she fainted. But not before she let out a scream that brought two of the other teachers running—and Mr. Weston, too. Someone said Miss Beckstead may press charges, Grandma."

"Oh, dear. Maybe you'd better wait in the car while I talk to Mr. Weston, sweetheart."

Hayley shook her head and molded herself to my side. I could tell that in spite of her apprehension, she wanted to give Braylen support as much as I did. She and her brother like to harass each other, but they're as thick as thieves when it comes down to it.

"Well, come on, then." I hugged her to me, bracing myself for the upcoming ordeal.

Mr. Weston's office door was closed. I could hear the low murmur of voices coming from inside, so I knocked. The door opened, and I could see my grandson and several of his classmates sitting across the desk from the principal. A uniformed police officer stood beside the desk with his feet apart and arms folded over his barrel chest. Several couples were present, and I assumed they were the parents of the other boys. Only Braylen's parents were glaringly absent and I thought to myself, Thank God the principal called me!

"Ah, Mrs. Thomas. Thank you for coming," said Mr. Weston behind steepled hands. "After I called you, one of the faculty members reminded me that Braylen's parents are on a field trip to the state capital as volunteers helping to supervise the three first-grade classes. They're due to arrive back at the school at any moment; meanwhile, we'll get started. Hayley, will you wait outside, please?"

"With all due respect, Mr. Weston," I said, "Hayley would like to stay if it's all right." I glanced at Braylen. His pale face regained a bit of color at the sight of a friendly face. Make that—two friendly faces.

"Very well." Mr. Weston cleared his throat and clearly and meticulously explained what had happened, based on eyewitness accounts and the frightened testimony of the five "delinquent" youths.

"These boys admit they didn't stop to wonder about the consequences of their actions. They agree that what they did was highly inappropriate and are willing to apologize to both Mr. Clark and Miss Beckstead. The problem is, Miss Beckstead has been unduly traumatized by the loss of her pet mice; in fact, at this very moment, she's lying down in the teachers' lounge with cold compresses on her forehead—and she's seriously considering pressing charges. That's why Officer Price is here."

I couldn't be sure, but I could swear Officer Price was suppressing a smile. I felt Hayley press closer against me and knew she was as frightened as her brother was. I looked around me at the austere faces

114

of the other boys' parents and blurted out, "Charges? What charges? These boys are only ten!"

A murmur spread through the room.

"Mrs. Thomas," said Mr. Weston. "I don't think you realize the seriousness of this incident."

My shoulders straightened. "Why don't you reprimand the boys—suspend them for a few days if you will—or give them after-school duties. I'm sure they've learned their lessons." I looked pointedly at my grandson. "You won't do anything mischievous like this ever again, will you, Braylen?"

"Mrs. Thomas—"

"I'll replace the mice," I continued. "I'll pay the damages and. . . ."

Just then the door opened and Andy and Tina rushed in. Andy was holding Sara, her face pressed tightly into the crook of his neck. My son and daughter-in-law stopped in the middle of the room and assessed the situation. Before anyone could stop him, Braylen sprang from his seat and ran across the room to his father.

After a moment, Mr. Weston broke the awkward silence. "Good afternoon, Mr. and Mrs. Thomas. Thank you for coming." He leaned forward. "Braylen, will you please return to your seat?"

With tear-filled eyes, Braylen beseeched his father. Then Tina, and finally, me. I nodded, and he reluctantly trooped back to his chair.

Andy whispered to me in an aside, "Mother, you can go home now—and take Hayley and Sara with you. We'll handle it from here."

"Yes," said Mr. Weston. "I appreciate your concern, Mrs. Thomas, but this is a matter between the boys and their parents."

Their parents! I thought indignantly. I'm more of a parent to these little angels than Tina could ever be! Why should I leave? I was on the verge of getting Braylen and his friends off the hook before Andy and his so-called 'wife' finally decided to show up!

"Trust me," my son murmured to me through tight lips.

"Oh, all right," I conceded. "Come on, Hayley. Sara." I lifted my youngest granddaughter from his arms.

Outside the office, the unfairness of it all swept over me and I almost retraced my steps. After all, I considered, I'm Braylen's grandmother; I've been his guardian for almost a year. Nothing like this ever happened while he was in my care! And now what does he face? Juvenile charges? A record of delinquency? Who will defend him and those other boys? Surely, not their parents! I was the only one present with the courage to speak up on their behalves—and I was asked to leave!

"Is Braylen going to jail?" Hayley asked in a small voice once the three of us were seat-belted in the car.

"Jail?" cried Sara. "Braylen's going to jail?" Her dainty features seemed to shrink even more.

"No. Your brother isn't going to jail," I said, but I wasn't so sure of that myself right then, to tell you the truth. Is it actually possible that they lock up ten-year-olds for such a minor offense? I wondered fretfully. "How would you girls like to go for ice cream?" I asked, plastering a smile on my face and forcing myself to act completely nonplussed.

Ordinarily, I knew they would shriek for joy, but my sweet granddaughters only looked at me in subdued silence.

"What did he do?" Sara asked in a tiny, timid voice, reminding me that she didn't know all the details. When I filled her in as much as I thought appropriate, she scrunched up her face and said, "Oooo. That's creepy. Snakes do that?"

"They don't know any better, dearheart. To them, mice are merely food." Smiling in spite of myself, I drove in the direction of McDonald's. Glancing back at my two darlings in the rearview mirror, I asked, "Haven't you two ever seen a snake digest its food on a PBS nature program?"

"We're not allowed to watch TV," Hayley replied, beating Sara to the answer.

"Not allowed to watch TV?" I asked, incredulously. "But—that's silly! What does she—I mean, your stepmother—hope to prove by keeping you from watching educational nature shows?"

Hayley shrugged dismally. "She says we should read good books, instead."

"We have our own library cards now, Grandma," Sara piped up proudly.

I steered the car into the parking lot next to McDonald's. "Well, yes. Books are wonderful." I turned off the ignition and turned toward the backseat. "And having your own library card is a very important privilege. But TV can be a learning tool, too."

What am I doing, I wondered suddenly, debating the merits of TV with my innocent granddaughters? Tina should be the one for me to argue with. I made a note of it on my mind's "to-do" list.

McDonald's proved to be not as much fun as it usually is. The girls sat quietly at our table and licked their vanilla cones, watching the other children play in the indoor McDonald's Playland. I knew they were brooding about their brother. So was I, wondering worriedly, What decisions are being made back at the school behind those closed doors?

That was the first question out of my mouth when Andy came to the house to pick up the girls later. I saw him park in the driveway and met him at the door, hoping the girls would stay absorbed in their

Walt Disney movie long enough for us to have a private, mother-to-son, adults-only discussion.

When I confronted him, Andy ran a hand through his hair—a mannerism he's had since he was a teen. "The boys were seriously reprimanded and suspended from school until Monday."

Good! I thought at once. Principal Weston apparently took some of my advice, at least! "Is that all?" I asked. "What about criminal charges?"

My son let out a deep breath. "No criminal charges. Miss Beckstead recovered enough to join in our discussion not long after you left. By then, she'd calmed down considerably, and she admitted that she may have spoken in haste. She said she knows the boys well enough to know they didn't mean any harm."

"Of course they didn't," I said. "They were simply being boys."

"Well, they're still old enough to know better, Mom," he said. "Otherwise they wouldn't have sneaked behind their teacher's back to do it." A hint of a smile played across his lips. "Anyway, I'm sure they'll think twice from now on before they get any more harebrained ideas."

"Oh? Why is that?" I could tell Andy was bursting to tell me something.

"Well," he drawled, "Tina suggested the boys hold funeral services for the mice, complete with eulogies, flowers, and prayers. Since the bodies of the mice are indisposed, Braylen and the others will have to make caskets and bury them in absentia. The entire class will observe the service."

Knowing how much Braylen despises mice after watching him help me trap a few, I was sure it rankled him more than criminal charges to be forced to think up eulogies and say prayers over the little rodents' graves. I smiled, thinking—for change, Maybe that daughter-in-law of mine has more on the ball than I give her credit for. . . .

"What about damages? Replacing the mice, for instance?" I asked. "I offered to make amends. . . ."

"You did? You shouldn't have, Mom. Anyway, Mr. Weston didn't mention it. It was decided that the boys will each contribute money to replace the mice."

"But Braylen—"

"Braylen will have to use his allowance, Mom. Or work to pay his share."

I stared hard at him. "Work? He's only a child, Andy! Is that another of Tina's brainstorms?" I looked past him at the empty minivan parked in my driveway. "Speaking of which—where's Braylen now?"

"He's home with Tina. Grounded."

117

"Grounded? On top of everything else? Besides, that's a silly punishment, if you ask me. Doesn't your new wife even have the good sense to realize that when grounding comes into play, the enforcer inevitably ends up being the one restricted? You never used to ground the children before Tina came along."

Andy's lips clamped even tighter. "Grounding Braylen was my idea, Mom—for your information." He looked over my shoulder and in a voice gruffer than usual, asked, "Where're Hayley and Sara?"

"They're in the family room, watching Cinderella." I suddenly felt silly for not inviting my own son inside. "Have a seat, Andy. Can I fix you something? A snack? A cold drink?"

"Not now," he said curtly. "Besides, didn't the girls tell you they aren't allowed to watch TV unless we're there to supervise?"

I glared at him. "Certainly they told me. But I hardly thought that ridiculous 'rule' applied to their time spent at my house. Speaking of which, Andrew—what is it with all of these rules all of a sudden? Isn't Tina going a little overboard?"

"It's not just Tina, Mother," Andy grated. "We're careful to keep a united front when it comes to making and enforcing family rules."

I flinched. Andy never called me "Mother." In retaliation, I said the first thing that came to mind. "Is that right? Well! I suppose if we lived during the Inquisition, you'd let Tina put my grandchildren on the rack or under the Guillotine!"

"Mother! What's got into you?"

Andy's scowl permeated my anger. I'd never seen him so irate. His face was beet red, the muscles in his neck taut, and he stared at me with steely intensity.

Maybe I went too far, I realized suddenly.

"I might be exaggerating a little," I said timidly, feeling somewhat reproached. "It's just that . . . Tina seems so . . . so heartless sometimes. . . ."

Andy continued to glare at me. "Have you even tried to get to know her, Mom?"

At least he was back to "Mom."

"Because if you did, Mom—you'd see for yourself and finally realize that she's anything but heartless! I've never known anyone to become so attached to three young strangers in such a short amount of time. Tina loves Hayley, Braylen, and Sara just as if they were her own flesh and blood, born from her womb." His voice softened. "They are her children now, Mom—don't you see? Everything she does, every decision she makes—it's all for their benefit."

I choked back a protest, wondering, Is Andy blind, for Pete's sake?

As if he'd read my thoughts, he changed his tone, obviously

118

to try to persuade me. "Tina's always careful to really listen to the children's side of things—and they can be little monsters out of your sight, Mom, believe me. Then she weighs the magnitude of their actions and approaches me with suggestions." His eyes shone with love. "For a woman who's never been a mother until now, Tina is uncommonly wise and fair. She never ceases to amaze me, Mom—honestly."

Hoodwinked, brainwashed, and bamboozled is more like it, I thought, but I didn't say anything. Andy could think what he wanted, but I had made my own observations over the past months.

As smooth as silk his face softened, and he put an arm around me. "You're a super grandmother, Mom. You'll never know how much I appreciate you taking the kids in hand when I was so messed up over Eileen leaving, but let's face it—grandmas can be total pushovers." He put a finger to my lips. "No, no—don't get me wrong, Mom; you're supposed to be a pushover. That's God's plan; it's all part of a grandmother's job description as 'God's angel in disguise.' But did you ever allow me to get away with the things you let your grandkids get away with?" He gave me a squeeze. "Just be glad you don't have to raise those little hellions. Okay? Lord knows, I sure gave you a hard enough time over the years."

Which wasn't true. Andy was always a model son. Well—except for the time he Super-Glued my best china to the table at Thanksgiving. And the time he filled wax punch containers with cod-liver oil and took them to school. And the time he drove the family car through the neighbor's hedges. . . .

I looked into his dear face. "I do seem to remember you delivering papers in the cold and snow one entire winter for breaking Mr. McConkie's grocery window with your boomerang. And I remember making you take piano lessons as punishment for pounding on the organ at church. You still play, don't you, Andy?"

He gave me a grudging grin. "Yes, and I even enjoy it. So you see, Mom—discipline isn't always a punishment; it all depends on how a person handles it. Discipline can be a teaching tool, too."

He was right, of course. If Tina truly loved the children as Andy claimed, I could breathe easy and not have to feel so responsible myself. As it was, I certainly knew that those three precious tykes needed a full set of parents instead of one parent and a backup grandmother. But I still wasn't at all convinced that a wicked stepmother wasn't abusing my three grandchildren.

"My 'perfect little angels' have become skilled at manipulating you, Mom," Andy continued, wrapping his arm around my shoulders. "It's time you and I—and Tina—work together to set limits and guidelines."

"But, Andy—"

He smiled a disarming smile and withdrew his arm from around my shoulders. "Oh, I don't expect you to quit spoiling your grandkids. That's a grandmother's privilege, after all. But they need to learn that family rules pertain wherever they are. Otherwise, they'll never conform to society's rules."

In spite of myself, I could see the wisdom in his words . . . even though I hated the thought of my precious babies being marshaled like Marines in boot camp. Then I thought about Hayley forgetting to babysit on occasion—and Braylen's mouth getting him in trouble with his stepmother. I even admitted how nice it was that Sara could tie her own shoes now and no longer chewed with her mouth open or chewed on her hair.

"Guess I'd better gather up the girls and skedaddle," Andy said, breaking into my thoughts. "Tina will be wondering what happened to us."

"You're sure everything is okay with Braylen?" I asked.

"He's plenty worried," he said with a shrug, "which just might make him think twice before he pulls such a stunt again. Don't you worry, though, Mom—he really seems genuinely sorry and he says he didn't know the boa would actually eat the mice. He learned two valuable lessons today: You don't play around with Mother Nature— and you don't show off for your friends!"

After Andy and his daughters left, I fixed myself a hot cup of tea and sat down to mull over what we'd talked about. One thing was certain, as far as I was concerned:

Tina really had the wool pulled over my son's eyes!

Well, he might be bamboozled, but that doesn't mean I'm going to drop my guard where she's concerned! My grandchildren mean far too much to me. And it's high time I stood up to her, anyway! In fact, I think I'll start by having the kids over more often. My house has already been like a mausoleum for much too long. . . .

The following day I called to invite them for a sleepover. In spite of my newly made resolutions, I was glad Hayley answered the phone and not her stepmother.

"Hello, dear. Halloween's just two weeks away, you know. How would you and your brother and sister like to come over and go through my old trunks to find something to dress up in?" As it was, I knew they always loved poking through my trunks up in the attic.

Hayley didn't say anything for so long that I thought she hadn't heard me. I started to repeat myself.

"I heard you, Grandma. It's just that, um, well . . . we're going to the mall tomorrow to buy costumes. We've been raking leaves to earn money for them. I'm gonna be Madonna—like from the Eighties."

Disappointed, I said, "Oh. Well, that's nice, Hayley, dear. Well, then—come over afterward, anyway. We'll pop popcorn and watch scary movies—oh, not too scary of course! Just the four of us."

Again, she hesitated. "Tonight? Gee. We've already made plans, Grandma. The whole family's going to Amazing Jake's." As an afterthought, she asked, "Wanna come?"

"No!" I said—too sharply, but my curiosity was piqued. "What is Amazing Jake's?"

She fairly bubbled with excitement. "It's a pizza place, and they have games, too—laser tag and miniature golf and even a video arcade! And a bowling alley, too! Plus a skating rink!"

Sounds like kid heaven, I mused wistfully. I almost wish I wasn't so quick to say no. . . .

"Who's idea was that, dear? Yours?"

"No. It was her—Tina's—Mother's." She stumbled over the words.

So! Tina has Hayley calling her "Mother" now, hm? How ever did she browbeat her into that? Then a thought occurred to me. "What about Braylen? Who's going to watch him while you're gone?"

"Oh, Braylen's coming with us."

"But I thought your brother was grounded."

Hayley stammered for a moment, and then said, "Tina—Mother—I mean, she's right here. Wanna talk to her?"

Indeed I did want to talk to Tina. Just what is her game, anyway, I wondered sourly. To think of the nerve—grounding my poor, innocent grandson and then backing down and planning a family night out! Did her earlier bluster interfere with her idea of fun? Hm! Just like I pointed out to Andy—grounding is as restricting for the grounder as it is for the groundee.

Tina came on the line. "Mother Thomas! I was going to call you. Do come with us tonight; we'd love to have you."

Oh, I'll just bet you would, I thought archly. I bet you had your hand suspended over the phone to call me, too!

"No, thank you, dear," I replied, my voice positively dripping honey. "But I'll watch Braylen for you if you'd like. Since he's grounded, you know."

"Oh, Braylen's grounding doesn't start until tomorrow. We've had this family outing planned for some time now."

"But aren't you contradicting yourself?" I asked smugly. "Andy was just here not an hour ago and he told me himself that Braylen is grounded."

"We have it all worked out," she explained. "Tonight's an exception because Braylen helped make the plans for Amazing Jake's. He'll be grounded an extra day to make up for it."

I gave a polite snort. "I see. Well, I guess I'm just too old-fashioned to understand this thing you young people call 'grounding.' The way I raised Andy, the punishment fit the crime. You know— back in those days, a child always knew exactly what to expect when he or she did something wrong."

After a stunned silence, she said, "Well, if you change your mind about tonight, give us a call. Good night."

Followed by a quiet click.

I went to bed that night convinced I'd won the first round . . . even though I lay awake until well after midnight feeling left out even more so than before.

The following week was interminable; it quite literally dragged by, giving me dirty looks the whole way! All I could do was think about how deprived my grandchildren were. I couldn't even turn on my TV without feeling guilty and doing a slow burn because Tina wouldn't "let them" watch their favorite programs. I also had vivid thoughts of Braylen, stuck in a corner somewhere—no doubt being fed little more than bread and water! He's always been so active, I fretted. I'm sure he's already at his wits' end. And there's simply no telling what other tortures those three little darlings are being put through!

I called every day to try and console them, but it was always Tina who answered the phone, and believe you me—she was like an iron buttress, even though she always sounded polite and congenial. I began to wonder if she'd forbidden the kids to go near the phone, too. I wouldn't have put it past her.

Finally, I got through to Hayley a week before Halloween. By then, I was as edgy as a pit bull on Starbucks.

"Is everything all right at your house?" I asked her.

"Oh, Grandma—you should come see! We've been decorating like crazy and our house is so cool! We're gonna have a scary party and you're invited!" She caught herself. "Oops! I wasn't supposed to say anything; it's a surprise!"

"A surprise?" I asked, suddenly suspicious, immediately figuring. Probably, Tina doesn't want me to come and told the kids not to mention the party to their grandmother.

"You won't tell that I told, will you, Grandma?" she begged.

"Of course not, dear. Mum's the word." No need to get Hayley in trouble with her overly strict, evil stepmother. I wouldn't put it past Tina to lock the girl in her room if she found out innocent Haley accidentally spilled the beans.

A Halloween party, hm? After Eileen left and before Andy married Tina, he and the kids always spent Halloween at my house to help pass out candy to the little ghosts and goblins. Now, suddenly, I just can't help feeling a pang. So many things have changed this past year. . . . I might as well be a picture in a scrapbook, for all I'm worth these days to anyone. . . . As it was, I wondered if I'd even get to see my grandchildren in the costumes they purchased at the mall.

In a pall of gloom I prepared for the upcoming holiday as though it were just another ordinary day. I stocked up on candy for the neighborhood trick-or-treaters, but my heart wasn't in it. After eating an early dinner of cottage cheese and pears—dinners were more bother than pleasure those days—I retired to the living room and switched on the TV.

When the first knock came just at dark, I picked up the huge bowl of candy and trudged to the door.

"Trick-or-treat!" cried a little, brown-haired girl with a backpack, a pirate with an eye patch—and Madonna, circa 1983—in unison.

I clapped my hands in surprise and delight at the sight of my beautiful, darling grandchildren.

"My, my! What have we here? Let me guess. You must be Polly Anna," I said to Sara, "and you're Captain Hook." I smiled at Braylen. "And Madonna must be in town on tour! What a pleasant surprise!"

"Oh, Grandma—but I'm Dora the Explorer," said Sara, obviously put out that I didn't recognize her favorite cartoon character.

I hugged them all and invited them in, glancing down the dark path to see where Andy was hiding.

He finally appeared with a shy smile. "Happy Halloween, Mom. We can't stay for long, I'm afraid; we just came by to get you to go trick-or-treating with us."

"I'll grab my coat," I said, not even bothering to run a comb through my hair. I wasn't about to pass up a chance to be with my loved ones on that hallowed e'en.

We drove the dark streets spattered with costumed children, and I wondered where Andy was taking the kids. One neighborhood is as good as the next for soliciting candy on Halloween, after all, isn't it? As we neared Andy's house, however, the realization hit me that perhaps we were, indeed, going to a surprise Halloween party—as Hayley had let slip several days before.

In fact, as I paid closer attention to my car-seated grandchildren, I could see that the youngsters were fairly brimming—near to bursting, actually—with the pent-up secret they were harboring.

Acting as though I suspected nothing, I let the two younger children lead the way up the path, through cobwebs and a dim, orange glow, to the house. Hayley trailed behind, catching my eye to remind me not to reveal "our secret." Placing my arm around her shoulders, I gave her a conspiratorial wink.

Except for an eerie iridescence, the house was dark and still. Where is Tina? I wondered suddenly. This was the first I'd even thought about my daughter-in-law.

Andy had parked the car in the driveway and came up quietly behind us. I expected some kind of explanation, but he didn't say a thing. He reached across the kids' shoulders and rang the doorbell. The door squeaked open, just like in the scary movies.

By this point, my grandkids were bouncing up and down with excitement. They'd dropped back against me and I wondered if they were scared, even though they'd helped create this "haunted house." Then suddenly, from out of nowhere, a weird apparition in a filmy shroud with a snow-white face and flyaway hair appeared. Startled in spite of myself, I assumed it was Tina. Sara screamed and backed closer against me. Braylen gave a half-laugh and looked from the specter to his father. Hayley and I simply gaped.

"Welcome to our lair," the person/creature/specter said, sweeping her hand in a gesture of macabre welcome. "But beware—the ghouls are restless and the vampire bats are hungry." A high cackle reverberated behind her. Even at my age, my heart thudded against my chest.

She was good!

Sara whimpered and buried her face in my stomach. Her little shoulders began to shake. Immediately, Tina swept off her wig and dropped to her knees in front of her.

"Sweetheart, it's only me! I told you I was going to dress up like Morticia while you were fetching your grandma. Remember, pumpkin? Don't be frightened." Gently, she stroked Sara's hair. "Come here; see for yourself, sweetums."

Sara unburied her head long enough to glance warily at Tina. Her sniffles subsided as she stepped hesitantly toward her stepmother. I held my breath, thinking, My daughter-in-law has gone too far this time.

I was just about to protest when a timid smile broke through Sara's tears. Tina gathered her in her arms and spoke to me above her head.

"Hi, Mother Thomas. Sorry. Welcome to our haunted house. You're our first guest!"

I choked out a, "Harrumph!" as my heart rate gradually returned to normal. "You plan on scaring all your guests this way?" I asked. I didn't mention that she'd scared me, too; after all—I was supposed to know better!

Tina laughed softly. "I guess not. I'd better tone things down a bit, huh? I'd hate to have all our neighbors run away screaming. The kids and I—and you, dear—" She smiled at Andy. "We all probably worked too hard to make this party a 'howling' success!"

Hayley and Braylen's courage had returned by then and they promptly pulled me into the dimly lit interior. Strategically placed

124

lighting illuminated the entryway and great room, which looked like a scene out of one of The Brothers Grimm Fairytales.

I stared in amazement. Great, hairy, black, loathsome spiders were suspended from gauzy webs in the corners; a skeleton clacked its teeth and beckoned from the doorway; flying objects, which I assumed represented vampire bats, darted to and fro; haunting laughter, spooky organ music, and eerie whispers sounded from dark recesses.

How ever did this young woman think up such a scene? I marveled.

I had to admire her imagination.

Tina let me soak in the atmosphere for a few minutes; then she grabbed my hand and said, "Come on, Mother Thomas—you need to get in costume before the others start arriving."

"Costume?" I pulled my hand back. "I'm not dressing up! I'm too old for such foolishness!"

"Nonsense, Mom," said Andy, pushing me from behind. "You'll make a great witch." He chuckled. "No insult intended. I told Tina about the time you dressed up for your Birthday Club Halloween Party and no one knew who you were! Remember?"

I preened, starting to get in the 'spirit' of things. "Well, I do do a great witch's cackle, if I do say so myself."

I let myself be led upstairs through the cleverly decorated house to a guest bedroom, where I donned a witch's costume. Tina complimented me, laughingly added a few finishing touches, and then took me to my station by the punch bowl—or, "witch's brew." The night went by all too quickly. People picked their way through the house in various stages of fright and amusement, ending up for refreshments in the dining room. Andy slipped a chair behind me and I became a "sit-down witch" in between guests and cackles. By ten, I was worn out, but I still can't believe how much fun I had! The children enjoyed the evening, too, immensely. And I grudgingly admitted that all of the credit had to go to my daughter-in-law.

I even told her so.

"Tina, this is the most fun I've had in ages." My voice was hoarse from cackling, but I said it heartfully, nonetheless. "Thank you so much for including me."

She smiled warmly. "Of course, Mother Thomas. We couldn't have done it without you—could we, kids?" She gathered the children to her and hugged them. To my surprise, they responded in kind. "Now, just imagine how much fun Christmas will be!"

"Can we go sleigh riding?" asked Braylen.

She nodded. "We'll sleigh ride on our tree-cutting outing."

"And caroling?" Hayley peered up hopefully into her face.

"Of course. And we'll make cookies and candy. You've all been so good with your chores and homework—we'll bend a few rules and make it a real holiday! The old-fashioned kind."

I peered at her to see if she were real; her enthusiasm seemed genuine.

Perhaps, I thought then, I've misjudged her a little.

Halloween was the beginning of a new relationship between my daughter-in-law and me. I could finally see then that, although Tina has her own methods of discipline, she's succeeded in drawing my three grandchildren to her and molding them into model youngsters without putting too much of a damper on their free spirits.

Now, when one of the kids tries to maneuver or manipulate dear, old Grandma with a tall tale of displaced justice, I sit them down sternly and ask, "Okay. So, now—what really happened?" It's paid off with increased respect for both their stepmother and me.

Today, as the holiday season draws ever nearer, I join in the activities and put my expertise to work when asked often ensconced in baking and candy making in the very center of Tina's kitchen, surrounded by love—and by my noisy, boisterous, wonderful brood. Mostly, I've learned to finally simply sit back and enjoy the busy, happy family life, content to be such a vital, loved, and blessed part of it all.

THE END

Made in the USA
Charleston, SC
03 December 2014